Nothing in the Basement
Advanced Praise

I thoroughly enjoyed *Nothing in the Basement*. I only got to it last night, but I couldn't put it down. It was a one-sitting read! Romie Stott's prose lures you into a seductive stranglehold you won't want to escape. *Nothing in the Basement* delivers a quietly intense exploration of a failing home and the true horror of an empty marriage. Plan ahead, and have your favorite security blanket ready because you're going to have a hard time escaping this story's grip.

- Trisha Trisha J. Wooldridge (New England Horror Writers Association), author of *Where Monsters Play*

Look at it one way, and Romie Stott's *Nothing in the Basement* is a sharp, occasionally ironic, scrutiny of two middle-class, middle-aged people, living in a money pit of a house at peak midlife crisis. It is also a story of the slow decay of environment, relationship, and sense of self. Domestic entropy, but make it haunted. Sometimes it was so startling or frightening, I gasped out loud. The reader seesaws between appropriately appalled sympathy and an odd schadenfreude that is so jubilant and malicious that it must come from without, not within. Surely this book has possessed us.

- C. S. E. Cooney, World Fantasy Award-winning author of *Saint Death's Daughter*

Nothing in the Basement

by Romie Stott

Dybbuk Press

2025

ISBN: 0-9766546-9-5
Long ISBN: 978-0-9766546-9-8
Library of Congress Control Number: 2025939661

Printed in the United States of America

Dedications

To Tom and Lisa, who (unwisely?) let me stay overnight in their house with a crawl space many years ago, and to Andrea, who said hello to a tree.

And to my sister, Arielle, the main audience for my ghost stories for more than thirty years. Vonnegut said every good writer is secretly writing to just one person, and his was his sister. Me too.

Chapter 1

Under the Brown house, there was an empty space. Sometimes it harbored a cord of hopeful firewood; sometimes workmen skimmed over powdery dirt to prod the house's underside. But most of the year, the space sat dark and untenanted, and the occupants of the house walked on an unseen apron of blackness.

The Browns were good people - comfortably overweight, generally honest. They worked in well-paying and socially conscious professions. They shopped at farmers' markets. They cared about good design so long as it didn't prevent them from hanging pictures of brides, wines, or their favorite cartoon characters. They were kind to their dogs without spoiling them. They were kind to each other when they were not frustrated. They felt patriotic when they paid their taxes. Often, they felt their taxes were too high.

Although they had moved into the house some time ago, certain boxes remained unpacked. They supposed they should go through these boxes, but they were content to simply raise the thought from time to time. Their names were Robert and Sandra.

Robert was in the parlor, kneeling next to a tarp, on which he had spread the innards of what would become a computer: he had spent a few pleasurable weeks selecting the components, a present to himself. He looked at the motherboard, and the gleaming screws beside it. He looked at the video card – a hunk of plastic, but exactly the right hunk of plastic, ready to be served by six extra-quiet cooling fans. He extracted the extra memory from its static-free sleeve. He felt like Doctor Frankenstein.

"Do you have to do that there?" asked Sandra.

"At this point? Yes," said Robert. "Why? Is that a problem?"

The corners of Sandra's mouth dipped in an expression that meant she was disappointed, but struggling to understand him. It was a dangerous face.

"I just wish you'd used the office – that's all."

"The office is full of dog hair," said Robert. "Not that it's dirty. The dogs aren't allowed in here, and it's out of the way. I'm just trying to be out of the way. Room to spread out, no chance you'll step on a stray screw, that sort of thing."

He smiled reassuringly.

"What I like about the parlor is that we don't use it," said Sandra. "If a guest comes over, I can take them to the parlor, and even if I haven't cleaned house – even if I didn't expect them – the worst the parlor's going to be is a little bit dusty. There won't be a forgotten coffee cup, or a stack of old bills, or a chewed-up toy. It's special."

"I'll be done in three hours," said Robert, although he privately hoped for more time. "Do you expect a guest in the next three hours?"

"No," said Sandra. "I don't know. My mother might stop by."

"Your mother of all people is not going to mind."

"I suppose. I just hate to see that tarp there. I can't look at it. I'm sorry." She disappeared to the back of the house.

Robert lofted each piece of computer and mounted it to the case. The components did not fit together elegantly. He had measured, but did that matter? Imprecision of manufacturing. Screws rattled in too-loose holes. To seat a circuit board required too much firmness.

Robert had the irrational suspicion that objects in the house could shrink or expand when exposed to the wrong mood. Electrons might keep their distance, or crowd together. It was all energy.

Impossible. He knew that. Sandra couldn't make screws feel small.

He retired to the bedroom to clip his fingernails. It was a constant aggravation between them, Robert was a healthy man with healthy nails. Sandra preferred to ignore this fact, and resented that she was not allowed to. It had led to many arguments, and finally a cold war - Robert clipped his nails at times and in places Sandra couldn't see, but then told her about it so she would know how considerate he had been, which defeated the point, as Sandra had to think about nail clippings. She filed her own nails. It was an aversion she could not explain. She was not troubled by the sound of Robert flossing. She found the occasional stray pubic hair on or near the toilet seat, and the insistent curve aroused a seldom-expressed tenderness.

"I don't like being made to feel I disgust you," Robert had said during one of their calmer but more deadly clashes.

"I can't help it. I'm not bothered when the nails are on your fingers. Unless they get too long."

"Well?" said Robert. Neither of them spoke for an hour.

Sandra thought of the conversation as she washed the dishes, which did not disgust her. She ran the water longer than she needed to, to drown out the sound of clipping, which she could not hear even when the faucet was off. She was being unfair. So was he.

Chapter 2

The dogs knew what was down there, and did what they could to get at it. Sandra viewed their digging and scratching as typical doggy mischief. She lamented the state of obedience classes. Robert asked the dogs "Are you hot? Do you need nice shade?" Sandra checked for chipmunks.

"There's nothing in there," she said to the dogs.

"Exactly," barked the dogs. "Let us fight it."

Sandra spent the day making plum preserves that didn't set properly. Robert took on the long-delayed job of painting the downstairs bathroom. Brush strokes on a wall of dried paint made him think of sugar frosting and poverty. To obliterate the rills and drips, he favored fine grade garnet sandpaper, followed by 230 fine and 320 extra fine.

Between waiting for the coats to dry, he tried to teach Pilgrim to play dead. His ideal was a situation in which he could walk away from Pilgrim, spin around, draw a pretend gun, point the gun finger at Pilgrim, and say "bang!" Pilgrim would fall down, and roll onto his back with his legs in the air.

So far, Pilgrim had mastered rolling onto his back. He'd taken to it almost instantly. Unfortunately, Pilgrim expected to be rubbed on his belly afterward. He would not play dead at a distance. It took an hour for Robert to discover this, because it took that long to stop Pilgrim from following him when he walked away.

"I think I used the wrong kind of sugar," mused Sandra.

Nothing in the Basement

"Did you try adding more sugar?" asked Robert.

"Or the wrong kind of pectin."

"I can get more pectin," said Robert.

"God, the heat on the stove could be totally wrong. It's not like I've ever used that candy thermometer against something where I knew the temperature. I should have tested it in boiling water. What's the boiling point of water?"

"100 degrees," said Robert.

"No - I'm not stupid. In Fahrenheit." Robert turned to Pilgrim.

"Bang," said Robert. Pilgrim rushed to the patio door, barking like a lunatic, knocking over a houseplant in the process.

"Pilgrim!" barked Robert, "There is nothing out there!"

"Nothing! Nothing! Nothing!" barked Pilgrim.

Chapter 3

On Wednesday, Robert spilled some gravy on the tablecloth just before guests came over to watch a favorite television show. It happened at the end of dinner - they were eating dinner before the guests arrived. The guests had not been invited for dinner. The spilled gravy didn't make sense. Robert's plate was nearly empty. To Sandra, it must have taken an effort of will. To Robert, it was mysterious. He was torn between overwhelming guilt and a growing sense that he had been set up.

"I'm so sorry," he said, scooping the gravy blob with a cloth napkin.

"Oh god," said Sandra.

"I'll put it through the laundry tonight."

"It has to be ironed."

"I will iron it," said Robert.

Sandra knew that saying anything further would not repair the situation. She took stock. There was no time to launder the tablecloth before guests arrived, which meant either using the winter tablecloth or leaving the table bare. The winter tablecloth would make her seem overly formal; what was comforting in cold weather became oppressive in warm. A bare table would look unfinished; the eye would wander from the bare table to notice small messes around the house - a cluttered spice rack, a crooked stack of cookbooks, a door frame that wasn't quite square. They would think that Sandra was unable to keep a house together. It would fall on her and not Robert. She tried to think of a way to move the table so that it was not visible from the front door, but the entire house flowed in and out of the kitchen. The table anchored the house. She would be justified in buying a more expensive table - something playful and artistic, with a classicism that would work effortlessly at a birthday or funeral. She needed more tablecloths, but not so many tablecloths that she became the tablecloth lady. Guests shouldn't expect a new tablecloth at each visit - not so many that she'd have to keep a chart. No seasonally themed tablecloths.

"Oh god," said Sandra.

Robert gathered up the tablecloth and put it in the washer, but did not start the washer. He didn't want it running when the guests came. That would muddle the television sound - especially the bass frequencies whose clarity was the main pleasure of a high-end sound system. Robert found Trixie's blue fuzzy toy behind the laundry room door, and he threw it to her a few times. She was delighted, but eventually her desire to fetch was not as strong as her desire to retain control. Robert went back to the washing machine, sprayed stain remover on the tablecloth, and returned to the kitchen.

"If we put Trixie in her sailor's outfit, and she runs to the door, I bet no one will look at the table," said Robert.

"You're brilliant," said Sandra.

Chapter 4

Sandra did not want children. Neither did Robert. It was not a source of conflict, except sometimes for Sandra. Nothing about the idea of childbearing appealed to Sandra - not the pregnancy, not the time off work, not the messes and tantrums. She didn't dislike children; she just liked other things better - the freedom to go to a bar after work, the lack of anxiety over a sharp-cornered desk. With adult friends, Sandra could ask whether she was too present or too absent; she could trust an adult to call her clingy or withholding and have it mean something. A child would not have a baseline from which to make this decision, and so the approval of a child would not bring the same reassurance. Other adults - especially other mothers - would know this about children, and prey on it. They could tell Sandra that she was a bad mother. She could say her child was fine, and they would say "how do you know?"

However, deciding not to do something never has the same definitive power as doing something. Decide to do nothing, and you could still do something, later, at any time. Nothing is not a choice so much as a constant choosing, an extended, deliberate energy expenditure rooted in "no." Every few months, Sandra had a crisis, and worried that she was negative, selfish, and delusional. She would see a baby, and she wouldn't be disgusted, but she wouldn't melt, either. She'd worry that some part of her hadn't woken up, and that it would do so just as the hot flashes hit, and she'd crave grandchildren, with no children to birth them.

Or she would visit her family, and have a bad time, and think, "shared blood does not mean you get along," and be glad. She wasn't stuck with eighteen years of caring for someone she was not certain to like. Who might be as dissimilar from her as her brother - her brother who had been raised in the same house. Then she'd freeze up, and think, "my god, I come from a dysfunctional family, and the fact that I don't want a child is evidence that I have not overcome it."

The temporary solution to Sandra's panics was usually money - either a transfer of money into her retirement account (a promise of comfort and adventure in her child-free old age), or a large donation to a carefully chosen charity - look at all the people I was able to help with money that might otherwise have gone to one child's trip to space camp.

Chapter 5

"I like a very clean vodka," said Robert as he perused the liquor cabinet.

"So do I," agreed Sandra and the guests.

"Some people think that if you like a clean vodka, you don't like alcohol, but I don't think that's the case. It's not as though I blend the vodka with heavy mixers. It's more that I like how little it tastes - how much attention I have to pay to it to notice the flavors."

"I know what you mean - it's like, red wine just hits you in the face," said one of the guests. "Anybody can notice red wine. You'd have to fight not to notice red wine. I don't think you could do it, even with your nose plugged."

"Exactly," said Robert. "Whereas with vodka - I mean a really clean vodka - I have to close down. I have to shut down my mind and just be with the vodka, and think about how I'm breathing. Imagine if you concentrated on water that way - you'd dry out. You'd shrivel into a little leather doll and die. But with alcohol, going so slowly is pleasurable. It shows self control and sociability."

"You can love alcohol, but not be a lush," said Sandra.

"You have to take your medicine," joked the guest.

"My ideal vodka would have no flavor at all," said Robert, "and it would be served at room temperature, so that all I would notice - no matter how carefully I paid attention - was the sensation of texture, the feeling of displacement as the vodka pushed through my esophagus, and the gentle effects on my biology as the alcohol permeated through membranes. I think I would like that very much."

It did not occur to Robert, Sandra, or any of the guests, that he had extended an invitation to the emptiness beneath the house.

Chapter 6

Sandra lost ten pounds in a week, without exercising or eating less. Without taking pills. She looked great. At first, she thought the scale was broken, but Robert tried it and weighed the same as the week before.

"You look great," everyone said, and it was just enough weight to make a difference. Her clothes still fit.

It worried Sandra.

"Why do I have to be such a worrier all the time," she chastised herself. "Why can't I think this is a miracle or good luck? I feel great. I was probably holding on to water weight because of stress, and I pissed it out once I relaxed a little, and now I'm stressing myself out, and it's all going to come back. I always do this to myself."

She worried that it could be uterine cancer, which was almost never found until it metastasized. She knew she was at greater risk for uterine cancer because she had not had a baby, although this risk was mitigated by her birth control pills, which in turn raised her risk for breast cancer. She wanted to go to a doctor and get tested, but she worried that she couldn't trust a doctor. So many doctors, men and women, seemed uncomfortable with the female reproductive system; they viewed it as treacherous or hysterical. Those in the former camp removed bits at the slightest suspicion. Just to be on the safe side. The latter gave out placebos and told women they needed to relax. Sandra did not want to be told to calm down, or to be more afraid. She wished there was a middle ground.

"Maybe this is early menopause," she thought, and that cheered her up for minutes at a time.

Chapter 7

The emptiness beneath the house had no thoughts or motivations. It wasn't. It galled the dogs, who were not Buddhists. When you dug a hole, you made it. A house was enclosed for some purpose. The nothing frightened the dogs because it helped no one and belonged to no one.

Chapter 8

On Saturday night, Robert and Sandra found themselves with the rare luxury of nothing to do - no dinner plans, no parties, no theater tickets. Plenty of food. Nothing on television. No take-home work, and no home improvement project they could plausibly complete. The dogs, astonishingly, seemed sleepy and uninterested in play. Robert retired to the garage, and the love of his mistress - a 1980 Triumph Bonneville with custom blue paint job. It was a flawless bike. Robert could spend hours buffing the thing. He often wished he had excuses to tinker with it, but it had always run perfectly, and the thought of taking it apart, of crippling it - just to get a slight and unnecessary bump to performance felt inconsiderate. Privately, Robert was anxious riding it; he wanted to protect his baby from the open road. The thought of a pebble scoring the pearlized hair of the hand-lacquered mermaid who winked from the gas tank made his heart squeeze down so hard it brought blood to his eyes. He stroked the chamois along the crash bar as gently and lovingly as he could.

"I won't let them hurt you, baby, my goddess, my Amphitrite. Not ever." He was talking to the bike and the mermaid and the idea of the bike and mermaid, and he felt foolish but he meant it.

Upstairs, Sandra relaxed in the bath with a large glass of red wine. She had not liked long baths as a young woman, mainly because she never got the temperature right for long, and partly because she hated the feeling of wrinkled toes. She didn't think bathtubs were designed to be comfortable. However, as she'd aged, she'd warmed to the idea of being a woman who bathed. It gave her an aura of luxury and sumptuousness. It was respectable, like smoking cigars or eating grape leaves. It was sexy without being sexual. And Sandra did feel sexy in the water; thighs she otherwise called fat seemed sleek and buoyant, like seals. (Swimsuits spoiled this effect utterly.)

More than anything else, baths afforded Sandra a chance to be alone without anyone assuming she was lonely. She could be alone without purposefully avoiding Robert or seeming like a workaholic. She could drink alone, and no one would call her an alcoholic. She thought of Robert at work in the garage. She felt mysterious, as though she was part of a club of other women and girls named Sandra.

Sandra had ridden a motorcycle every weekday from her fifteenth birthday until she graduated high school. It hadn't seemed like a lifestyle choice - just a way to get between home and class, one she could afford. In college, she'd lived on campus. Afterward, she'd had office jobs, and the business suit of an upwardly-mobile executive was not so forgiving of road dust.

Sandra had not mentioned her motorcycle to Robert. He liked the bad boy fantasy - the idea - he was pushing an envelope. He liked to have a hobby, and a garage to retreat to. Sandra liked that she could give him this. And it pleased her to know that should she need it, there was a well-polished Triumph waiting in the garage.

She'd been a good swimmer once, too - not a lifeguard or a racer, but faster than friends who were lifeguards and racers, at least when it came to the crawl. She'd climbed trees and thrown rocks into creeks, and done all the tomboy things. She had a collection of coins in the attic. Nothing valuable. Just pennies run over by trains, nickels with holes in them, fifty cent pieces, and a treasured Italian Lira. For years, she'd looked at them before a test, or when a tooth was loose; jingle the box and think "Yes I can have things."

Drowsily, she thought she should show Robert - it was exactly the sort of thing he could get enthusiastic about. He'd take it too far and tell everyone and give her more coins. Maybe she should dig out some paper dolls instead.

Sandra inhaled a lungful of water, and it so surprised her that she tried to inhale again. She grabbed the edge of the tub and held herself up. Her body jerked around, and she coughed. She couldn't get air.

It went on too long. Her brain started counting the tiles on the wall, but it kept getting lost, and the tiles moved. Water went into her eyes.

Robert ran in and lifted her up. He thwacked her on her back. She couldn't do anything. Eventually she breathed; he wrapped her up and put her in an armchair.

"When I first came in, I thought you were bleeding," he said. "The water was colored."

"I dropped the wine," Sandra said.

"It's a good thing the door was unlocked," said Robert.

Am I getting that old, Sandra thought, to fall asleep in a bath after half a glass of wine? The thought of a similar incident without Robert's rescue terrified her. The terror and anger were much greater than her gratitude to Robert.

Chapter 9

One of the local churches regularly ran 30-second ads during Robert and Sandra's favorite sitcom. This had prompted Robert's endless speculation. Clearly he and Sandra were a target demographic - educated people who had strayed from the church when they left for college, but who might now have children. Possibly the ad spots were cheap; the show's following was devoted, but small.

"It bothers me that most religious people seem to believe that atheists don't think about God," said Robert.

"Mmmm," said Sandra.

"There's this whole idea that maybe I haven't thought about it or maybe I do believe in God, but am angry at him and therefore pretend I don't. 'I'm ignoring you, I'm ignoring you.' Well, I have thought about it, and I am certain there isn't a god. I am not angry at him because he is not real."

"Yes. I miss the choirs, though," said Sandra, who often played Christmas music even in the summer.

"I mean I'm not angry at the tooth fairy, or Santa Claus, or Superman. I just realize that they're fictional. I don't think I'm less of a person for it. God, I have so much wonder. It's so moving that life exists, and that we can perceive it, and that Pilgrim's nose works the way it does. I don't think it's better to say that some invisible angry man controls it, while playing tricks on dumb little me. I think people should be nice to each other because it makes for a better society, not

Nothing in the Basement

because the angry man who can do anything wants it. I would go to church if they would just stop bringing God into it. We could take communion and remember everyone in the world and everyone who has ever lived, and we can talk about morality and amazement. Just not God."

"And death shall have no dominion," said Sandra.

"And we can read Dylan Thomas," said Robert.

"No," said Sandra. "I mean death. I mean you have to have magic god, or else what happens when you die? You just go away? It's random, and the good stuff didn't matter and the bad stuff didn't matter and you're nothing? That may be true, but I don't want to look at it every week. That's why God. Otherwise, it's just too hard to think about."

"Are you kidding?" said Robert. "I find the idea of being forgotten *very* comforting. I like going into a graveyard and seeing a faded headstone I can't read. I like it better when it's half covered in ivy and I might not find it again. I like knowing that unless I'm really awful - really awful *and* really powerful - nobody's going to remember what I got wrong."

"What about the stuff you go crazy to make great," said Sandra.

"We're on a tiny planet in a giant universe that will end eventually. Nothing is that great, and there is no reason to make myself crazy."

"Well I don't want to die and be nothing," said Sandra. "I believe that's what will happen, but that's not what I want. And that's not what I want for you, and that's not what I want for the dogs. Your science church is going to have to come up with some comforting fourth-dimensional workaround, or I'm not going."

"Hey hey hey," said Robert. "I still love you for eternity, and I wish you wouldn't talk like that."

"Well, say a little prayer," said Sandra. "And stop trying to out-atheist me."

"Hey," said Robert.

Sandra went to get ice cream and ate it sullenly. They watched the rest of the show.

Chapter 10

On Monday, Robert's front teeth fell out. It happened when he got out of bed. He sat up, and felt them wiggle. He pressed them with his tongue, and the teeth landed on his lower lip. Robert was not frightened. He had first lost his front teeth at age eighteen, while playing hockey. He was, however, perplexed. Dental bridges were meant to last ten years, and his insurance allowed a replacement every five. His current bridge was two years old. The unseated teeth were completely clean - no trace of dental cement. He leaned close to the mirror and saw smooth gum bookended by tooth pegs - little filed-down stubs equally devoid of cement. Had it dissolved overnight? He had eaten no food, drank no drink, and produced little saliva.

He phoned his dentist. He phoned the emergency number on his dentist's answering machine. Could this be a super bug? Were other members of the dental community suddenly struck? He imagined multiple mouthfuls of un-moored braces. His dentist called back and said to come in on Thursday. Use Fixodent until then. Robert called into work and said he'd be late. He worried that his consonants sounded soft. At an unfamiliar pharmacy, Robert purchased a small tube which promised flavor neutrality. He kept his mouth closed during checkout. Once he was safely in his car, he read the instructions carefully. He correctly applied the fixative, and the bridge stuck. No excess fixative pushed its way out.

Nothing in the Basement

The fixative tasted like tired horses, aluminum foil, aspartame, and backlight.

At work, he didn't smile. He talked as little as possible, and tried to breathe through his nose. He took the stairs rather than risk sharing an elevator. He worried that he smelled old and would accumulate other geriatric smells, like stale sweat and old urine. He was very careful when using the bathroom. Overly careful. He blotted. He checked for signs of underarm wetness, because he had read that dental adhesives could render your nose useless. He drank a smoothie for lunch.

He sent Sandra a message: I understand everything. I miss you.

Sandra wrote back: Thanks?

He wrote: Don't kiss me tonight.

Chapter 11

"You look awful," Sandra's mother said.

Since her parents' divorce and her mother's re-identification as a lesbian, her mother had embraced brutal honesty. She was a straight talker, unafraid to cut through the bullshit. When you didn't care about the subjects, it was fun. A relief even. Sandra liked to see her happy and fulfilled, but sometimes Sandra wished her mother had not been so thorough in throwing off oppressive 1950s strictures. The two were lunching in her mother's new favorite place - a dive bar that served only German beer and pepperoni pizza, with décor from Christmas 1985. Sandra's mom said it was 'authentic.'

"No I don't," said Sandra. "I'm just under a florescent light, and you're looking for excuses to worry."

"No," said her mother. "You look tired."

"Well, I'm not," said Sandra.

"Okay, okay," said her mother. "Suit yourself." She picked at a coaster and waited to see whether Sandra would follow up with an outpouring of everything bad in her life or at least a good confession. She intended to wait until she received this confession, but she got impatient.

"People can paint their houses the color they want," said Sandra, although privately she thought she'd be discomfited by a neon green house or even adobe pink. Her street was mostly beige. The brightest house might attract extra traffic, and the type of people who had parties every week, with parked cars on both sides of the street. She didn't even mind the idea of drug dealers, if only they were discreet. Maybe that was racist.

"Don't be racist," she said.

"Well, I think it's wonderful," said her mother. "Such a happy color to look at every morning. I went over and talked to them, and do you know what they said? They said they got the idea in Amsterdam. Can you believe it? The Dutch have these round blue houses. I can't even imagine. They have two of the most adorable little girls - you should meet them. I'll introduce you next time you come over. We should take a trip to Amsterdam, just you and me - leave Robert and Kathy behind. Wouldn't that be fun?"

The idea of a vacation from Robert sounded unexpectedly pleasant. Exchanging him for her mother held less appeal. Her mother sensed her hesitation and misinterpreted it, no doubt deliberately.

"Or, oh, not Amsterdam. Paris. Or Cancun! Wouldn't that be funny. Or London - you've always loved London. Remember how much fun you had at the British Museum?"

Sandra's main memory of the British Museum was her 8-year-old declaration that she loved Roman ruins - proclaimed loudly, while looking at parts of an Egyptian temple. Everyone had been very amused, and the story had been much repeated to relatives at home. It had been a perfectly sensible error - the kind only an intelligent child can make. She knew the Romans had once ruled England; the Egyptians never had. These must have been built to honor Caesar's wife, Cleopatra. She had been very proud to figure it out, and it had been a powerful lesson in the ways life cheated.

Nothing in the Basement

"Listen, sweetie," said her mother, "are you sure you're all right?"

"I'm fine," said Sandra.

"How's Robert?"

"He's fine."

The pizza arrived. Her mother ate half, and forced her to take the rest home. Sandra steered conversation to books her mother liked - biographies of royalty, mostly - and let her talk.

"All that dynastic turmoil makes me glad to be an American. I do like the clothes, though - as long as someone else is wearing them." Her mother pushed back from the table as much as was possible in a vinyl booth. "I know you think I'm just meddling, but are you happy in that house?"

"Yes," said Sandra. Her mother looked away.

"It just - I guess it's not what I expected. For you. I would have guessed it was someone else's goal. People get trapped in a house. Women get stuck. Let me buy you another beer."

"Mom, I need to get back to work," said Sandra. "And I love my house. I love knowing that I don't ever have to move again - that I can put something in a drawer and not have to find another place for it unless I want it to move. I love having stupid dogs that run around in the yard, and I love picking up pine cones, and I love having a guest room. I love that house more than anything in my life. I'm not going to leave it unless it kills me, and even then, I want to be buried in the back yard. Next time, find something else to worry about, okay?"

"Sounds like a trap to me," grumbled her mother.

Chapter 12

Robert arrived home to find that the dogs had shredded cushions throughout the house. "Bad dogs," he said, and shut them in their crates before he began the arduous process of surveying the damage. As he moved from room to room, his mood darkened. The shredding was comprehensive. It was also focused. Each shredded object was Robert's, from his bed pillow to the sofa cushion where he most often sat. Suspicion immediately fell on Trixie, Sandra's dog from before the marriage. Trixie had always been friendly to Robert. He spent more time feeding, grooming, and playing with her than Sandra did. It was, he suspected, a key reason Sandra had trusted him early. Perhaps some buried part of Trixie had resurfaced - a hitherto latent identity as the guard dog of a woman living alone. Or maybe it was his smell; he put a hand over his mouth.

Chapter 13

Sandra had watched a nature special some years before. A zoologist had explained animal tracking, including how to make guesses about an animal based on its spoor. Carnivores had long, snaky, continuous excretions; herbivores left piles of soft round pellets. Ever since, Sandra had examined her bowel movements, and judged how they tallied with the previous day's proportion of meat to vegetable. She liked the brief excuse to think about how her body worked and moved and made energy; she liked to think of herself as an animal, because she liked animals. (She often watched on-line videos during work hours, and forwarded the cuter examples to co-workers.) In the bathroom, in front of the toilet, she forgave herself. Then she flushed.

Lately, the act of flushing had taken on a certain suspense, and justified Sandra's special attention. Thus far, the house's toilet had responded well to plunging. It would need a good snaking soon. Sandra only put it off because she dreaded what else a plumber might recommend. The waterworks of an old house held mystery and power in the same proportion as her reproductive organs. One could either ignore them or blame them for everything. The idea that the plumbing might ever work perfectly seemed ludicrous. Most workmen made her feel guilty - either furious with herself for agreeing to work she didn't believe in, or nervous that she was bullheaded, stingy, cynical, and oblivious to risk. As she plunged, she plunged the rhythm of TMI. Plumbers and doctors gave too much information about systems she couldn't control. A cause without symptoms was no cause at all. Expert talk about causes always struck her as men showing off - a display of power and entitlement. As much as Sandra disbelieved all forms of women's intuition and the magical power of mothers, she had to admit that they worked as a bulwark against the flood of male expertise. You want irrational? I'll show you irrational. I can do magic, and you can't even tell.

The sound of Sandra's plunging carried into Robert's dreams. It hadn't made sense to him to go into work for the few hours before his dentist's appointment. He was snoozing luxuriantly, even though he knew gradual waking only made him sleepy and low-spirited for the rest of the day. In his dream, Robert was trying to drive a car out of a flood - a blue 70s-model Citroen with a sticky gearbox. He had to divine the road from landmarks - avenues of trees, the top of a hydrant, the hump of a mailbox. Sandra sometimes sat in the passenger seat, quiet and pale, hands tight around a precious object. At other times, she was gone. Dark water obscured the surface of the road. When Robert drove over something, it shredded his tires and crippled the car. He could neither see it nor guess what it was.

The emptiness beneath the house had no thoughts or motivations. It worried the dogs. When you dig a hole, you make a hole. A house was enclosed. The nothing frightened the dogs because it helped no one and belonged to no one.

Chapter 14

The dentist could not explain Robert's decoupled teeth.

"Could it have been a problem with the batch of dental cement?" asked Robert.

"Could be," said his dentist.

"Or maybe I ate something and it reacted somehow. Maybe I'm constantly eating or using something, like baking soda in my toothpaste, or acai juice - it's in everything now; you can't escape it - or bergamot, and it's been slowly dissolving this whole time, only the cement adhered so well that everything stayed secure until it was all gone."

"Could be."

"Then how do you know it won't happen again?"

"I don't think it will," said the dentist.

"This has been very embarrassing for me," said Robert.

"How about if it falls out again, I'll fix it again, free of charge?"

"Well... I'd still rather it not happen." A weak joke. The dentist smiled, but he smiled out of politeness. The dentist made some notes.

"Do you think it's the motorcycle?" asked Robert.

"I do not," said his dentist.

What the dentist did say was that the x-rays showed bone loss unrelated to the trouble with the bridge, and that Robert needed to floss more carefully and use prescription fluoride toothpaste. Maybe come in for another checkup in three months to see whether a periodontist needed to get involved. He pointed out on the x-ray where Robert's roots didn't go so deep - "that's nothing you're doing wrong - it's just how your teeth are, and it puts you at greater risk than some people."

He drew circles around small dark pockets below the ghostly image of gum line, places where Robert's jaw was receding.

"I wouldn't worry about it, though," the dentist said. "Just keep an eye out."

When Sandra got home, Robert met her with a big smile and a picnic basket. This was a risk - she did not like most surprises. She was delighted. They piled the dogs into the car and drove to the park to watch the sunset while Pilgrim ran after squirrels. When Sandra curled up against Robert's shoulders, he felt taut like a hot air balloon, filled with pride and half a bottle of wine. He'd made all good choices, from the right salad dressing to the decision not to talk about the dentist. (The jaw pockets would only worry Sandra.) He was a god.

"We never do stuff like this anymore," said Sandra. "What brought this on?"

"I love you, and I think it's crazy that we don't do things like this anymore. Why not be newlyweds forever?"

Sandra snuggled in closer. Another right answer. In his head, Robert floated above the countryside. The grass below spelled out an infinite scoreboard, full of his initials.

Chapter 15

For the next several days, Sandra made a special effort to wear makeup and good lingerie, but quickly lapsed into old habits. She couldn't say why. It only took an extra ten minutes. She could've switched to instant oatmeal. But after putting makeup on, she would worry the rest of the day that the makeup had gone wrong. She checked mirrors obsessively. She was convinced that sweat or rain would dissolve her mascara into raccoon eyes, or that lipstick would smear into the small wrinkles around her mouth. This had never happened to Sandra, nor had she seen it happen to anyone else.

She supposed she'd gotten the idea from an old movie. Perhaps if she saw the scene again, the fear would go away. Or get worse. In any case, she worried about what would happen if she forgot to wash her face one night - not just breakouts, but makeup layered over makeup. She looked at pictures of Queen Elizabeth the First. She imagined pressing a finger to the white face paint. She imagined sinking in. When she got up in the morning, she splashed her face with water, once, and that was that.

It was not a time of year for walking out of doors. Too hot. Too many mosquitoes. Only tolerable on the patio, seated, with a cool drink. Moving made your blood pump. Sandra tried not to wear shoes in the house. She kept plastic gardening clogs by the front door. In practice, she only wore them to walk down the driveway and pick up the paper, in blessed early-morning cool.

It bothered her to have to get the paper. Was it so hard to hit the stoop instead of the driveway? It was the same distance from the road. She suspected Frenchwomen dressed to get the paper and did not dread the idea that a neighbor might start a conversation. It felt stupid to wear a robe in the summer. It felt stupid to wear clothes at all. There was the usual speculation that men would turn into ravening beasts under the influence of a full moon. Men should control themselves. Clothing in summer was nothing but decoration.

Sandra was jolted from her usual internal rant with the discovery that she was locked out of the house. Out of distracted reflex, she had twisted the button on the inside of the door handle. That damn thing. She walked around back to bang on the patio door, and she started to feel gravel - first one stone inside her shoe, and then others. She raised her feet higher - she actively did not shuffle - but the pebbles kept coming. She couldn't work out how they made it over the side of the clog. She looked with incomprehension at the hole worn through the ball of the sole, which had been perfectly thick only moments ago. She could have sworn. She did swear. Cheap shoes - what could you do? The manufacturers were crooks.

When she reached the patio door, Robert did not answer. Nor did the dogs. Likely all were in the basement for the morning feeding. Just in case, she heaved against the locked door, feeling ridiculous. She broke a sweat almost immediately. She tried to be patient.

There were smears on the patio glass - dried streaks of cheap cleaner, slobber from dogs, and spatters where bugs and birds had flown. Taken together, they formed an outline of a tall, thin person, watching her. Then it seemed the shape was behind the glass, moving through the room. She heard a loud crack.

A tree slammed into the house and two roofing tiles hit her.

There was no wind.

"Just time of year, I expect," one insurance adjustor said as they examined the damage. "These trees don't live forever. They get rotten in the middle, and when the hot weather comes..." He shook his head. In his opinion, the damage was not structural. It would require just the attention of a roofer. The deductible was not high.

"I were you, I'd throw in a little extra if it meant getting it fixed quick," the adjustor said. "You want it fixed before it rains. Unless someone else got you covered for floods."

"We will," said Sandra.

Chapter 16

"I think Death would be a conservative chess player," said Robert. He and a friend were sitting in their favorite Irish pub, enjoying Guinness and wood paneling. They had been there since just after dinner, and intended to remain until the bartender closed shop for the evening.

"Nah," said his friend. "He'd be aggressive. What does he have to lose? You don't die then, he's just going to get you later. If I were Death, I'd play chaos chess."

"I guess it depends – do you think the chess part of being Death is more tedious, or the rest of it? You'd spend so much time around people who were old or mangled or sleeping, I think you'd be delighted to have a conversation with someone sharp enough to challenge you. Even a bad chess player – you wouldn't want to off them immediately. Let's face it – you're better than they are. You've played millions of games. Even a grand master who played a dozen games a day didn't play as many games as Death plays in all of time."

"When was chess invented?"

"Modern chess? Like the 1200s or something. Real spectator sport – lots of bets placed."

"My problem with this theory," said Robert's friend, "is that it assumes that all experience is good experience. Your hypothetical grand master has spent a lifetime playing grand masters and strategic computers and so forth. Death has an eternity, sure, but against the best players? He's playing whoever happens to challenge him. Half of them could be

36

kids. Maybe they've never even played chess before. Sure, Death thinks he's good, like I might think I was a good tennis player if I was in a league full of gouty septuagenarians, but if Nadal walked in? No way. Death probably tries some cocky bullshit because he expects everyone to be worse than him, but it's a skewed sample. You probably just have to be slightly above average, and, bam, you blow his skull."

Robert ordered another round. As he waited at the bar, he ran his tongue back and forth across his teeth – an old habit to remove red wine stains. Somehow, it had become an alcohol reflex. He returned and set the glasses down with the weight of a gavel.

"You're wrong," he said, "and here's how I know you're wrong. Death can stop time. He stopped time to have the chess match. *He is holding the chess match outside of time.* You don't think Death can stop the time outside of time, teleport to any library anywhere, and read a relevant chess book? He can model a whole simulation. If Death loses, it must be because he finds it funny."

"Why the chess game at all, then?" said Robert's friend. "Why not just reap the soul and have done?"

"Table talk."

"You don't think all-powerful Death could have a conversation with whomever he wanted to?"

"I don't," said Robert. "I think if Death showed up, you'd freak out. He'd offer a chess game, and you'd assume it meant you were dying. Which come to think is maybe something he does sometimes, and those are the people that quote-unquote beat him. I think the chess game, dying or not, is a prop to relax people."

"You think chess is Death's 'Apples to Apples.'"

Nothing in the Basement

"Dust to dust." They sat in silence for a few moments, making amused faces at the neo-Celtic harp music that blasted from behind the bar. They had competing theories as to what the bartenders listened to in their off times – Robert thought Bauhaus; his friend thought Coldplay – but agreed that it was not folk revival.

"I just had a sad idea," said Robert's friend. "What if you beat Death and live forever so you can be a companion to Death? Like, he set up the chess game as a test to find someone who could get him to stalemate – an equal. And his idea was to make the equal immortal so he wouldn't be afraid of him. But of course that kind of thing is not the way to make a friend."

"Mmmmm," said Robert. "I think you make a good point that Death is lacking in social skills. But I think stalemate -"

Robert's phone played the ring that meant Sandra. Robert rolled his eyes theatrically, then smiled.

"The house has exploded," said Sandra. "Please get home as soon as you can."

Chapter 17

Sandra was enjoying a girls' night. Her sorority sisters - those who still lived in the area - were splayed across couches, drinking various strengths of gimlets. They'd never been a proper sorority so much as a group of salacious bookworms, but one of them had realized that with official status came free use of campus facilities, and occasional funding for costume parties. They were the only class of Kappa Alphas; they'd never rushed another girl. They'd graduated with closed ranks and a dead charter. Robert had thoughtfully made himself scarce for the evening, disappearing to a bar Sandra hated with a friend Sandra tolerated, and a promise to be home no earlier than 2:30.

"God," said Blue Sweater In Summer, "I've been married so long now that I'm starting to think even talking to anyone else is cheating on my husband.

"Awww," said Tank Top and Ethnic Jewelry, who had remained single. "That's sweet."

"I mean it," said Blue Sweater. "It's freaky. It's like he's filled my emotional and physical needs for so long that it feels wrong to want anything from someone else. I would do everything online, if it was possible. Leave it outside the door, thank you."

Chic Black Sundress laughed. "Well, I can't wait to have an affair. Seriously! I would have done it already, only I haven't found anyone suitable." Sandra believed this was possible. Since Black Sundress had been diagnosed with breast cancer (thankfully in remission), she had regularly sought out scandal. It wasn't a zest for life exactly – more a ploy to get people to think of her as something other than a woman with early-onset cancer. Sandra sympathized. Black Sundress continued.

"I mean, I love my husband more than anything, love him, but our life seems awfully non-bohemian. If one of us had an affair – it could be him – just to embrace the zest and fullness of life ... I'd be jealous, I admit, but I think it would make me feel young. All that backstabbing in college. As long as we were still kind to one another. Why aren't we all an enclave of despicable British colonials sleeping with each other and being cruel to horses? I blame all of you. I also regret that none of you has a sufficiently dashing and caddish husband."

"She has a point," said Comic-Con T-Shirt – Sandra's favorite Kappa Alpha, and the one she was least close to. "Most psychiatrists now recognize that there's a chemical component to love, or at least to romance. A dopamine reaction." (Sandra wished she could lead off a sentence with "most psychiatrists now recognize" and sound authoritative rather than ... sort of pompous and desperate. She knew also that the same Comic-Con t-shirt would *not* look similarly insouciant and with-it on her; she'd look pitiably out of touch.)

"Well, no wonder liquor helps!" said Tank Top.

"It's not like alcohol, though," said Comic-Con. "It's like, maybe, heroin. You build up a tolerance after a few years and that sort of dizzy passion falls away to something quieter. I don't miss it, myself. I hate chase games."

Nothing in the Basement

"How depressing," said Blue Sweater. "Like love only exists to get you through nights up with a toddler and then your brain doesn't care."

"I think it's kind of nice," said Sandra. "It takes the pressure off."

"Oh, well, of course you'd say that. You and Robert. I like to think of you and the dogs curled up in bed in the morning. It makes me feel cozy. It really does." Tank Top smiled. "It's really sweet."

"Oh, you have no idea," said Sandra. "The other day, a tree attacked me."

"Inside the house?"

"It did its best," said Sandra. "Field trip!"

The women crowded onto the glassed-in patio to giggle and harrumph at the not-yet repainted patchwork of ceiling repairs.

"You should have seen what it did to the roof," said Sandra. "I'm an idiot – I should have taken pictures."

"And you were sitting right here?" said Tank Top.

"I wish," said Sandra. "I was outside, maybe two feet away. I got hit by tree shrapnel. At six in the morning. No scars," she added.

"Thank goodness none of the glass broke."

"God," said Black Sundress. "Remember back – what – seven years ago? Some kind of tropical storm drove a fat tree limb right through my bedroom. I remember, it's the stupidest thing, I was in my kitchen, and I heard a loud noise in my bedroom, and I swear to God, I said, 'Hello?' To the tree. And then I had to try to cram garbage bags around the hole to stop water coming in. I can practically hear it now."

"No. I can hear it too," said Comic Con.

Nothing in the Basement

"Jesus. it's probably the upstairs toilet," said Sandra. "Just a sec."

Just then, the women started to notice the unpleasant smell not quite like ammonia and raw pork. The stench was worse in the kitchen. When Sandra opened the door to the basement, it was overpowering. The dogs began barking and whining; she could hear them scratching at the door of the upstairs bedroom. She flicked on a light. The basement steps didn't reach the floor. They ended just six steps down. At that point, an implacable mass of what must be raw sewage interrupted the descent. It wasn't brown. It reminded Sandra of calves' brains, and she would no longer shop at certain Southern convenience stores. Calmly, aware of her guests, Sandra waited to see if the liquid level would rise. To settle herself – to feel in control – she tried to describe the smell to an imaginary reporter. She found herself totally at a loss. The scent words she knew applied to wines and perfumes. Juniper. Oak. Tobacco. The best she could manage was tangy and cabbage-like, but that also described coleslaw.

The shitlake was not rising. She was very sure. It cut across the bottom of a picture frame, and did not move further up the stem of the picture's stylized expressionist wine glass. She realized with terror that she'd nearly shut the dogs in the basement. That was what she usually did. She didn't know why she hadn't tonight. She thought of the dogs stuck beneath the pungent surface, ribbons of mush packed into their fur. She felt weak. She thought she might fall; she imagined plunging into fetid oatmeal. Warmth radiated up at her, volatile and sinister decomposition. She wondered whether the smell would be worse if shit filled her nose, or whether it would act as a plug.

Nothing in the Basement

She clamped her mouth. Her dizziness frightened her. She felt she was going to fall. She'd been wrong to flaunt her freedom from vertigo, all those times on cliffs and tall buildings. She did not want to touch a wall. It felt as though the essence of shit had coated every surface of the house on a molecular level. She was going to fall.

A friend put a hand on her shoulder to steady her. Another handed her her phone.

Chapter 18

The dogs were asleep in the car. Robert and Sandra sat at a booth in an all-night diner.

"But there has to have been a noise," said Robert. "It couldn't just appear."

"I'm telling you there wasn't," said Sandra. "There was a trickling sound, and then immediately a smell, and then it was there, all of it." She sipped heavily-sugared coffee – not her usual style.

"How loud were you girls talking?"

"Robert."

"Was it really more of a whoosh?"

She eyed him. He plowed on.

"I'm sorry. But we're talking water through a seam in the Titanic, here. We're talking blood splashing out of an elevator in *The Shining*. Were there splash marks on the walls?"

"I don't know. I don't think so. It was – it was a very even level. Entrenched."

"Well, did you get a good look? Are you sure?"

Sandra looked at him hotly.

"I said I don't know. I didn't head down the stairs for a closer look."

"Well. Okay," said Robert. Sandra knew he was thinking she should have, when she was damn proud of how she'd handled herself. She thought of saying, "well why don't *you* go back and look," but she didn't.

They waited until eight in the morning to start calling plumbers. Once they found one who'd work on Sundays, they went home to wait for him. They didn't haggle on price.

Sandra worried that she'd been wrong that the flood had halted, or that it had started up again, and overnight the house had filled up while they were selfishly away. When she opened the front door and a wave of shit didn't roll out to meet her, she wanted to cry. Subdued and silent, she trailed Robert to the basement, although she wanted nothing more than to take a shower. She realized, with fear, that it might be dangerous to run any water, though she recalled it might run through different pipes. Robert gallantly descended three steps to make room; she tried to follow his example. With a stern but inquisitive frown, he surveyed the damage. *He's a good man*, Sandra thought.

For the first time in his life, Robert began to admire port-a-potties, and the powerful chemicals they used to keep shit-stench at bay. He'd thought they smelled awful, but now he saw that they were masters of sensitive discrimination. The thick gray scum in the basement smelled nothing like a well-maintained outhouse, and nothing like the fresh diaper of a colicky toddler. It smelled boggy, stagnated in the rotting process, untrammeled from both chemical and natural decomposition. Robert felt queasy as he recognized small identifiable pieces of corn.

"It's funny," he said in as even a voice as he could manage. "All of this is human waste, but it doesn't seem human. It seems like poison meant for an alien species." He paused. "It feels like inorganic matter bubbling up from an alternate universe."

Nothing in the Basement

Sandra threw up. It didn't make the smell worse. The color was almost cheery in comparison. Robert took her elbow and led her onto the lawn. It didn't escape the smell, but it put it at a distance. He tried to imagine how the sludge would look outside of basement gloom. Things always looked better in daylight. He pictured a moist gray crust of dissolved toilet paper and half-digested food, spread across the entire earth, six inches thick. He pictured it on top of snow. He pictured it dry and cakey in Death Valley. He pictured it undulating above the Pacific. He sat down very quickly and didn't stand up until well after plumbers had stomped through the house and dragged hoses through his front door. And even when he stood, he waited before moving.

Chapter 19

"Oh, it can do that," said the plumber. "These sewage pipes can back up real fast if they break. Once the top of the leak is covered, the liquid muffles the sound."

"And it just stops like that?" said Sandra.

"Oh yes. It reaches its level, you see, where the pressure is equal. Like those fancy dog dishes – you know what I'm talking about?"

"No," said Sandra.

"Like sea level," said Robert. "Without tides."

"I guess," said the plumber. Sandra screwed up her mouth. It wasn't like sea level, and damn Robert for acting like it made perfect sense when he'd told her all night it wasn't possible.

The plumber double-checked their address and said that he and his crew would be back to patch up tomorrow and he'd send an invoice by the end of the week. He did not say that it had been a full day of hazardous, unpleasant work, but they knew that it had. It would cost at least ten thousand dollars.

They wrapped their shoes with plastic grocery bags and trudged down to the basement. The plumbers had pulled up carpet only in the area where they'd been working – the rest of the floor was still soggy. Sandra had no idea how to dry the carpet, or get rid of it. She supposed she should call the city health department, but felt an irrational fear that they'd condemn the house.

Nothing in the Basement

Robert marveled at the broken pipe. It had burst through inches of concrete, as though it held a fire cracker. A pipe bomb.

"I don't think a pipe should even be down there," he said. "We're eight feet underground. The rest of the pipes are along the ceiling. It seems like an odd choice."

"Oh what do you know about houses," said Sandra.

The pipe in question had connected their house to the municipal sewage main – the line that connected the house's many small tributaries and carried them to mingle with their neighbors' runoff in a contained shit river under the street. Sandra thought of it all rolling past and felt crazy for living nearby – like she'd built a shack on the edge of a hurricane beach. The backup was not the city's fault – the plumber had been sure of that. He'd told them with real sympathy, knowing it was not reassuring.

If the city was to blame, the city might pay.

No such luck. The burst line was theirs, privately, and whatever blocked it had flowed from their house. Things didn't flow in the other direction.

Only they did, Sandra thought, *into our basement.*

Nothing was dry. The carpet squelched underfoot. Sandra saw puddles. The wall below a certain height was no longer cream, but uneven khaki drab, flecked with semi-dry pieces of stringy matter that looked alarmingly close to pet food or tuna. There were human hairs much longer than hers or Robert's. She was tempted to grab one for evidence, but she knew she didn't have the energy to start that fight.

"What are we going to do?" she said.

"Well," said Robert, "I think for tonight, we should close this place off, and go upstairs and open windows and light smelly candles. Tomorrow, the crew will bring industrial fans, and they'll dry this stuff out. We'll make some decisions when we've slept. I'm not up to thinking right now; are you?"

"No," said Sandra.

The next day, the plumbers brought fans and shop vacs, and the basement got drier but not really dry. In the evening, it started to rain, and Trixie bit Robert, which she'd never done before. She didn't break skin, and they agreed she was overexcited, and confused. Because of the rain, they couldn't put her out, so they shut her in her crate, and listened to her whine all night. Sandra was glad the roof had been fixed.

Chapter 20

"We have to do something," said Sandra. After days of rain, the sun was back, and the air was miserable. They'd switched off the air conditioner; all the house's windows and doors were open. Box fans were spread across the basement. Sandra lived in a cloak of bug spray.

"Give it a few days," Robert said. "This is the first chance it's had to dry out, and I want to know how bad things are before we start bringing people in. Maybe we can do it ourselves. Those repairs cost a hell of a lot of money."

It was at this point that Robert made the mistake of rereading *Heart of Darkness*. He had made a resolution to better himself intellectually by reading at least one great work of literature a month. To make things easier on himself, particularly with the stress of the house repairs, he thought he'd start out slow - not *War and Peace*, but something short – something he'd studied in college, already owned, and remembered as having good action scenes. It seemed the best way to carry on through a difficult patch of life.

Upon his rereading, he discovered that the explosions had been from *Apocalypse Now*, and the world was a senseless place of creeping horror. He lost all ability to confront the aftermath of the flooded basement.

Sandra tried to make a list. She knew that once she laid down the total of what was lost and what might be

Nothing in the Basement

recovered, the details would stop rattling in her head. The trouble came from boxes of family photos, which she had brought down from the attic to sort and scrapbook. She tried listing them as "photos – 3 boxes," and then "photos – 2 large boxes and 1 medium box," and then "photos – 12,000? plus negatives," but remained unsatisfied. She started to list subcategories: Aunt Betty's photos. Wedding photos (Beth and Alex). Wedding photos (honeymoon). And then individual photos: "Third birthday party. Blue dress by mom. Chocolate cake on my face. Mimaw in background."

It made her crazy – crazier than if the house had burned down.

The ruined photos were Robert's as well as Sandra's, and she supposed he must also have strong feelings - must feel hopeless over the loss. In this context, his delays might spring from depression, or caution. Sandra had trouble holding on to these thoughts; they seemed like a Robert she had invented. The real Robert was like a stove that could heat and cool as dials were turned, but didn't sit there thinking. Sandra knew she must be wrong, but, in crisis, she couldn't maintain the fiction of a Robert behind the face of Robert. It made her feel lonely and angry. He got to have a vote in the household?

At night, they closed the windows, turned on the air conditioner, and tried to pretend the house didn't smell like a gas station toilet. On the third night, the air conditioner did not turn back on.

"Why did it do that?" said Sandra.

"I don't know," said Robert.

"Is it bad to turn an air conditioner off?"

"I don't think so."

Nothing in the Basement

They stared at one another. They opened the windows again, and lay in bed, sweating. Robert spoke into the darkness.

"You know, air conditioners were invented to kill humidity," he said.

"What?" said Sandra.

"Air conditioners. They were a sort of dehumidifier. The cold air – that's just a bonus. A convenient emergent behavior, you could say."

"That doesn't make sense. You're making this up."

"No, seriously. It's a dehumidifier." He could feel a dip in the mattress as Sandra switched position.

"Where do you get this stuff?" she said.

"It's the kind of stuff I know."

There was silence – good silence. Then Sandra laughed.

"Who says, 'ignore the cold air, hot people – think about the *dehumidity*.' 'Hey – here is this glass box that projects pictures; we think you might like the way its static electricity lets you collect dust in one place.' That is so stupid."

"It really is," said Robert.

The emptiness beneath the house had no thoughts or motivations. It galled the dogs. When you dug a hole, you made it. A house was enclosed. The nothing frightened the dogs because it helped no one and belonged to no one.

Chapter 21

Robert woke up, freezing cold. His first thought was that the air conditioner had come on with a vengeance. His second thought was that he was running a fever. He heard liquid hitting liquid in the master bath, but couldn't guess whether it was vomit or diarrhea. Sandra crawled back into bed, teeth chattering. Robert clumsily brushed his knuckles along her hip.

"This goddamn house," she said.

"It's probably food poisoning," said Robert. "Or flu. It feels like food poisoning."

"What do you think food poisoning is?" said Sandra. She moaned. She rushed back to the bathroom. Robert's stomach felt blocked. Making it downstairs sounded noble but impossible. He pawed at the waste basket. At the first eruption, Pilgrim padded over. Robert's second puke just missed his friendly head.

For the next three days, neither Robert nor Sandra was able to keep down even a glass of orange juice. Sandra systematically bleached the entire kitchen and boiled all their drinking water. By the third day, she looked like Nosferatu – stiff elbows, hunched shoulders, and black moons under her eyes. Robert had better luck sleeping, but he wasn't good for more than washing towels. They lay in bed and watched sports – any sport. Anything talky and unimportant. When the hosts replayed slow-mo versions of the highlights and re-announced the score, Robert felt understood.

"I need soup," Sandra said on day four.

"Can you hold it down?"

"Depends on the soup."

"Is the soup magic?"

"Yes."

"I will bring you this soup."

Robert staggered to the kitchen and banged a pan on the stove. He pawed through the refrigerator for vegetables that looked easy to digest, rescued a misplaced shaker of parmesan, and pulled jars from the pantry until he found an orphan bouillon cube. He laid his head on the table and let the vegetables boil until they disintegrated, then sluiced the broth to an aluminum coffee mug. (Sturdy. Would not break when dropped. More usually reserved for the morning commute, but it seemed unlikely.) He plopped in an ice cube and a powdery heap of parmesan.

"I know I should sip this, but I'm just going to chug it and hope my body doesn't notice," said Sandra. "I think I heard something like that from a sports coach – the basketball one. Here goes."

"Wait!" said Robert. "Shit." He grabbed the glass and poured it down the bathroom sink. He trudged back downstairs, and returned with another mug, not quite as full.

"I'm sorry," he said. "That wasn't parmesan. That was oven cleaner. I'm so sorry."

"Jesus," said Sandra. She set the cup down, and looked at it suspiciously. "Oven cleaner? What the fuck?"

"It was in the fridge. It was a green cardboard tube with a shaker on top."

Nothing in the Basement

"What the fuck was it doing there?" said Sandra. Her voice was breathy and tumbling. "It goes under the sink."

"I know," said Robert, soothingly. "You must have put it there by accident when you cleaned. You were kind of delirious."

"I didn't use the oven cleaner," said Sandra.

"Maybe you just moved it."

"I could have died," said Sandra.

"I stopped you in time."

"What if you hadn't stopped me in time?"

"You would probably have thrown it up."

She looked unconvinced. "Why didn't you smell it?" she asked. "You were in the kitchen a long time."

"I didn't cook the parmesan – just added it at the end. And I can't smell anything – just bleach and the basement and pumpkin spice candles. I could eat a raw onion and not know it."

Sandra deflated. "I'm sorry," she said. She reached out to Robert, and he patted her back.

"It's a good thing I stopped you," said Robert. "Imagine if I hadn't."

"I don't want to," said Sandra.

"It's funny," said Robert. "I could totally have gotten away with it – I mean poisoning you. I'd get off scot-free."

She stiffened. "I thought it was an accident."

"That's exactly what it would look like! The loving husband makes soup for his wife. He's a little bumbling – he's sick, too! He's that devoted. Couldn't even smell over the bleach. Innocent as a lamb."

"I thought you said I'd just throw it up and be fine."

"The wife keels over, how tragic, poor guy. He must feel awful. And the best part is, she poisoned herself. *She* cleaned the kitchen. <u>She</u> put the cleaner in the fridge. It's practically an O. Henry story."

"This is not funny," said Sandra. "At all."

"You're lucky you have a husband like me, who is so smart and caring. Somebody a little more hesitant would retire to the Bahamas with a fat roll of life insurance."

"I don't have life insurance."

"Yes you do – through my company. It was cheap."

"Don't talk to me," said Sandra.

Chapter 22

On her first day back at work, Sandra was welcomed with a rant.

"It's disgusting," said her office mate. Sandra immediately checked her blouse.

"The billboard," her co-worker clarified. Sandra looked blank; the woman rolled her eyes. "The billboard. The. Billboard. Did you honestly not notice? I've been calling all day to complain."

"What billboard?"

"The one out front – the one with the body on it."

"What?"

"I know. Exactly. Disgusting."

"What?"

"Suicides. Murders."

"Over a billboard?"

"On the billboard. That's what it says."

Sandra felt that somehow, she'd gotten off the wrong train. The hidden cost of sick days. It had been a tactical error not to stop for coffee. Surely, she could have found a way to juggle purse, laptop, keys, and cup. As soon as she settled, she was a magnet for re-hashed gossip – out of the loop. Dropping things off at her desk had been a foolish luxury. It would take days to make up missed work with the interruptions.

"I'm sorry," said Sandra. "The billboard?"

Nothing in the Basement

Her co-worker settled in, fluffing herself like a peahen.

"It's for a forensic cleaning service. They come in and clean up bodies – murders, suicides, old people who croak and go undiscovered for days. Sure, it's a service, I can't deny it – but do I need to think about death on my morning commute? Use some euphemisms. Have some decency. You know?" She tossed her head for emphasis. "Who needs an ad for that, anyway? You'd think the police would tell you. I've been calling all week to complain. I hope I've tied up their phone lines. I hope they're afraid to answer the phone. I wish I could do more, but I have to do my job, you know?" She sighed.

"What's their number?" said Sandra.

When her co-worker left for lunch, Sandra dialed, careful to muffle the mouthpiece from imaginary snoopers. A professional-sounding young woman answered.

"*Do you clean up shit?*" Sandra hissed into the phone.

"Lady, stop calling," the young woman said.

"No! Please don't hang up. I mean it. Do you clean shit – I mean, human feces? Not from a dead person?"

"Organic waste is organic waste. How much crap are we talking? Kid with behavioral problems smeared up a room, or I need to bulldoze an outhouse? We don't do that one, but I can rec someone."

"Just a – a flooded basement. The, um, the waste isn't there anymore, but it's on the walls, and in the carpet."

"That," said the woman, "that is what we do. How big a mess?"

"Big. Very big. And do you do – not just rooms, but stuff? Papers? Covered in feces?"

"Oh yeah. It's expensive, but yeah." Sandra could hear that the woman was smiling. "Lets us pretend we're archaeologists. May I ask how you heard about our service?"

"The billboard," said Sandra.

"Love that billboard," said the woman.

Sandra pulled money from her 401K, took the tax hit, and booked them for the following week.

"This is a lot of time off," said her boss.

"That was sick leave," said Sandra. "This is a personal day. It's allowed."

"This is not a good attitude," said her boss.

Robert was angry, too. He was unmoved by Sandra's desire to pay for the problem and make it go away. Their money versus her money didn't change the principle. He wanted to wait and see how much their insurance would cover the plumbing. He thought the mess and misery worked in their favor.

"It's not covered," said Sandra. "Floods are not covered."

He stiffened his back to seem as tall as possible.

"This was not a flood. This was a structural defect. We'll get a news crew into that basement, and we'll see what they decide to cover."

"Well, the cleaners will be here next Tuesday," said Sandra, "so I guess you should hurry."

Chapter 23

The forensic crew turned out to be a family unit – a brother and sister and two cousins. It hadn't started that way – it had been just the brother, transitioning from lower-paying janitorial work. He'd found out it was a good gig – paid better than construction. Fewer hazards. Gradually, as positions had opened, he'd gone through back channels to talk up out-of-work relatives – anyone who wasn't squeamish. It was now a family business not owned by the family. ("Don't need the stress," said the brother.)

As a result, the atmosphere was unexpectedly festive – a combination of morbid humor and fraternal pranks. Sandra was issued her own loaner face mask once it was clear she'd be in the basement for the duration. While the cousins sprayed down the walls and pulled up carpet ("cheaper to replace than salvage," they'd said, as though there might have been another possibility) and hauled wrecked furniture to their flatbed-secured dumpster, the sister and brother sat at a folding table, flicking photos through a chemical bath and flash-heating them dry - a process Sandra didn't understand.

"Nice to be in a basement," the sister said. "Dark. Lots of room. Good for photo recovery."

"Nice bangs," the brother said to a permed prom portrait of Sandra.

Nothing in the Basement

When the crew's lunch break came, Sandra surprised herself by offering them all beers – and not cheap beers, but good ones.

"This is a real nice house you've got," said the stocky cousin, who had immediately befriended both Trixie and Pilgrim. "Reminds me of someplace. Hey – we been out here before?"

"I don't think so," said the sister, who Sandra belatedly recognized as the woman on the phone. "It didn't come up on the computer."

"Huh," said the cousin. "It's just real familiar."

Three hours later, he snapped his fingers. "Murder-suicide," he said.

"Oh shit," said the weedy cousin, who had shifted to expanded photo duty. "You're fuckin' right. Front stairway. Son of a gun."

"Don't listen to them," said the brother. "A lot of houses in this subdivision have the same floor plan. It was probably blocks over."

"Oh, yeah," said the stocky cousin. "Didn't mean to scare you. I meant it was this house – not that it was *this* house. Lord, that one could keep you up at night."

"What happened?" said Sandra. Her voice sounded funny behind the rubber mask. The smell in the basement was a tenth of what it had been, but she wasn't taking chances.

"Oh, just a domestic dispute," said the weedy cousin. "No kids, at least. That's a hard situation."

"I think I was in Florida for that one," said the sister. "That the one where they're having an argument, he shoves her, she falls down the stairs, breaks her neck? Then he hangs himself, they're both found weeks later by a Jehovah's Witness looking through the mail slot?"

61

Nothing in the Basement

"No," said the weedy cousin. "Different one. More ragey, more premeditated without being premeditated. No clue why, but he tries to bash her head through the slots in the banister. That shit's sturdy wood, and it doesn't give, but he keeps mashing. Makes a real mess of her skull. Blood all up and down the stairs. Brain matter. He gets the head halfway through – bastard actually manages to pack it into that shape before he gives up. I kind of think, why stop there – you're committed. But he stops there. Thank God, she's dead at that point – her head had swollen after that, they'd've had to cut the wood to get it out. Shame to lose a damn sturdy banister on top of everything else." He looked seriously at Sandra. "These houses may look the same as those pieces of crap across the highway, but they're nothing similar. Good construction you got. I'd hold on to this." He bent back to his work.

"And the man died too?" said Sandra.

"Now that I think of it, I don't remember. I think – I remember it as being murder/suicide, but I don't remember cleaning up after him. Died tidy, I guess."

"This is a real nice story," said the brother.

"Aw, shit. I'm sorry," said the cousin. "I'm real sorry. I lost track of myself. Shit."

"It's okay, said Sandra. "I asked."

The mood was subdued until quitting time. Sandra agreed to trust the remaining photos with the crew.

"We'll get 'em back to you by the end of next week," said the brother.

"Thanks," said Sandra. "Hey – really. You saved my life."

"Eh, it's our job." He smiled. "It's why we do it. We brag, but it's not really about the *dead* people."

"Doesn't that stuff get to you, though?" asked Sandra.

Nothing in the Basement

"It's no worse than what you see on TV these days," said the sister.

Chapter 24

Robert spent half the day convinced that his hairline was receding. He checked different mirrors and different lighting conditions. He took photographs with an arm's length digital camera. He read Wikipedia articles and tried to remember pictures of his mother's father, who had died in some kind of sordid convenience store shooting - probably died too young to have revealed balding tendencies. His own father had been bald as a cue ball, but this was only relevant insofar that Robert had loved him very much, and never once missed his hair.

One of Robert's great regrets was that his father had never truly met Sandra. Robert had barely begun dating her at the time. They'd touched in a flurry of kissed cheeks and shaken hands at some non-intimate family event.

"Is she a smart girl?" his father had asked. "Can she keep up with you?"

"She's pretty smart," Robert had said. "She writes press releases for large corporations. She's really good at it." Robert did not know, and had not known, enough about press releases to know how exactly Sandra was good at her job, but one could not remain in the field without talent.

"Is she a happy woman?" his father had asked. "Does she make you happy?"

"I think so," said Robert, remembering that when she laughed he felt as though he was doing a wonderful job at

Nothing in the Basement

life. He wanted to live in that moment. She fought him for the last glass of wine or the last slice of cake. Previous girlfriends had never done that – not even girlfriends. His former wife had made a show of giving him the best of everything, and then held it against him.

"Hold on to her," his father had said. "If you love her, then fuck it. Nothing in life is easy, no matter who you're with. People talk about the love of your life. I'm old, and I'll tell you – one way or the other, you're alone. If you can be alone with someone smart, and she makes you smile, then hold on to her. That's my advice."

Two months later, his father had had a stroke, and ten months after that, his father had died. He had since avoided his mother and older sisters as much as was practical. Without his father, they didn't feel like family. Nevertheless, he called his mother to ask about hairlines. He was that troubled.

"Mama, was granddaddy bald?" he asked. "How about your mother's father?"

"My mother's father? What kind of a question is that?" said his mother. She sounded snugly drunk, as expected – likely bourbon mixed with Dr. Pepper. "I loved your grandfather. He always bought me candy on Sundays. Always. No matter what. That was love. Nobody had anything." She took a swill of something. "Are you going to talk some sense into your sister?"

"Probably not. Who? What's she doing?" Robert realized as he asked that he did not want to know.

"She wants to get rid of your father's suits! Donate them to the homeless or something. Talk to her. She pulled them all out. They're in a pile in the living room. I chased her off, but she'll be back. As though I –"

Nothing in the Basement

"It sounds like a pretty good plan, mama."

"Those suits are for you, Robbie," his mother wheedled. "Your father had them specially made. He would want you to have them. You don't want a stranger walking around like he's the man your father was. Those people are –"

"I'm not the same size as him, Mama," Robert said. He did not add that the suits were off the rack, or that his father, whatever his other excellent qualities, had a deep love of synthetic fabrics.

"Oh, things can be taken in," said his mother. "A good suit is a good suit. You're so rich you can throw away money, but in my day –"

"Mama, you were born middle class in a time of national economic prosperity, and Daddy's waist was twice as far around as mine. I could make two pairs of pants from his pants."

"That's good thinking," said his mother. "Come over tonight, before she takes them all away."

"Mama –"

"'They're not going to fit,' 'They're not going to fit.' Stop being so negative. Like you need an excuse to come see your Mama. Bring Sandra." The line went dead. Robert's mother did not answer when he redialed. He took the small revenge of letting the phone ring more than twenty times. His mother still refused an answering machine. Thought it was cold.

He took off early from work and drove to the older suburb where his mother lived in a house that was too big for her. The extra bedrooms had never made sense. He and his sisters lived within a half hour's drive. It had been a mostly unsuccessful play for grandchildren. Robert's nephews and nieces demanded she travel to *them*. Then they could rely on the tactical fallback of movies and video games. For brats, they were pretty smart.

Robert's mother opened the door with a big smile that fell immediately.

"Where's Sandra," she said.

"Oh, you know," Robert lied, "she has that class she takes the dogs to – the obedience class." While Sandra was very nice about Robert's mother, they had an unspoken agreement that Robert would limit her exposure. "I actually can't stay long – dinner plans."

"Well," said Robert's mother, "those dogs certainly need some discipline, but you would think she could make the time. I suppose she's just following your example. Why don't I get you a Coke?" She bustled to the kitchen in a swish of disapproval. Robert spent the next half hour making perilous small talk that veered between his sisters, their husbands, and their children and the ingratitude of his sisters, their husbands, and their children. He made a point of checking his watch "unobtrusively," and did his best to convey a sense of urgency - a sense of "I'm terribly busy but I'm here smiling because I love you but I have to go anyway and it's tearing me apart." When he finally saw an easy means of extracting himself –

"I won't keep you any longer; I know your talent show is about to start -" (she was addicted to the heartwarming stories of scrappy young American performers trying to make it. She resented that none of her children had so much as twirled a baton)

"I don't know why you avoid me," his mother said, theatrically dabbing her eyes. "You act like I killed your father, when all I did was feed him. And even if I had, it's still no excuse. I never held it against *my* mother." Robert didn't bother to react. *Here we go*, he thought.

"Mama," said Robert, "Granddaddy was shot in a convenience store."

"Well, yes," said his mother, looking smug. "By your Gramgram."

Robert heaved a sigh at the trap. "How has this never come up before?" he said. "Is this another 50-miles-in-the-snow we-had-it-so-hard story? You can't just make things like this up when you want attention."

She set her jaw. "Your Gramgram shot your Granddaddy. In a convenience store."

"Where did she get the gun?" said Robert.

"Her purse," said his mother. "This was Kansas. You don't know how dangerous things were."

"I don't believe this," said Robert. "Why didn't she go to jail?"

"She was a woman! She had small children! Women aren't like men, Robbie. They don't just kill people without a good reason. That's not what women are like. They'd really much rather make a nice home, be pleasant. I worry about these girls who want to go into the military. What kind of boys have they been running with that like a girl like that?"

"The feminist movement really passed you by, didn't it," said Robert. "Leaving that aside, what was Gramgram's good reason that kept her out of jail after shooting a man in a convenience store?"

"He was shoplifting," said his mother, as though this was obvious.

"Mama, I've got to go," Robert said, standing.

"Don't forget the suits!" said his mother.

On his way home, he dropped them in a Goodwill bin – all except a paisley tie he might wear as a gag.

Chapter 25

Sandra wasn't even sure she had a library card.

She did, however, subscribe to her local newspaper. She logged on to the archive, where she searched various combinations of "murder" and the names of nearby streets. She turned up an unsettling number of hits before she found the staircase case. It had indeed been a few streets over, although the specific house number wasn't listed by the paper. Later, she would drive down the street, scanning for a house that looked like hers. When she found it, it had green trim, and a basketball hoop on the garage. A starter family had probably gotten a deal – murder houses went cheap. Sandra wondered if neighbors avoided the house. She'd always believed, to some degree, that violence left a psychic residue – free-floating trauma to haunt anyone who walked too near. She liked to imagine that horrible things affected more than the direct victims; it seemed less lonely. She liked to think someone somewhere paid a penance– even if it was an innocent person who had unexplained nightmares. It was, deep down, the reason she read the news. But this house looked happy and safe.

The paper was less clear than the cleaners on the subject of suicide. There had been a gun in the basement, laid out beside its lockbox, with his and her fingerprints. It had not been fired. After he had bashed his wife's head in, the husband had left in his car, and crashed at breakneck speed

Nothing in the Basement

into a streetlight, killing himself instantly. Immediately after pulling out of the driveway, he must have floored the accelerator. Complicating factor: he wore his seatbelt. The investigators had later discovered that he was tens of thousands of dollars in debt; the bank was about to foreclose. Those interviewed said that the wife had not known, or had affected not to know. The day before, she'd treated her friends to lunch.

The police were not interested, once they confirmed who had killed whom. The couple involved hadn't been rich or attractive enough to sustain a publisher's forbearance beyond a few local interest stories. Sandra was left to turn the puzzle in her mind, insoluble. Had the wife seen it coming, or had it come as a complete surprise? Had the husband been fine one minute, gone mad in the next, returned to sanity afterward? Had he built up a rage? Had she egged it on? Had she discovered his debts? Had he discovered her largesse? What about the gun – unfired, but loaded, and out of the box? Had something started in the basement? Had he meant to kill her down there? Had the banister death come from a botched escape, or panic? The banister was next to the front door.

That night, Sandra found herself pacing her own basement, trying to think it out. Perhaps they'd made a suicide pact, but she backed out. Perhaps he'd meant to kill just himself, and she'd discovered him and gently pried the gun away. She'd promised him comfort. He'd followed toward the bedroom, but when he reached the front stairwell, he realized that nothing in his life had improved. She loved him but didn't know his problems. He was mired in the same humiliations. Overcome with despair, he had turned to crush the closest living thing.

Nothing in the Basement

Or the un-boxed gun could be a coincidence. No law said they had to put it away. They didn't have children. Outside the box could be the gun's natural state. He might have forgotten he had it; not everyone used their basements. Sandra realized she was staring at the spot where she would place a gun – and was surprised to discover that her brain had sorted through the possibilities. The basement had a gun spot. Never mind that Sandra owned no gun.

The floor molding in the gun spot had pulled away from the wall. Specifically, it pulled away from the side of the stairwell. The wall looked like the rest of the basement, but was built up of drywall and plaster.

Shit, she thought. Doubtless the wood had warped after so much exposure to water and heat. There was only one way to judge the damage – whether just one board needed to be replaced, or whether opportunistic mold had impregnated the understairs. She grabbed the nearest straight sturdy object and levered the board loose.

Behind the board was a smooth expanse of wall, with the pencil-scrawled words "There Is No Home Here." Sandra's stomach felt as though it was filling up with cold liquid. She went upstairs and stayed with the dogs until Robert came home, her back to the wall.

Chapter 26

"It's just a joke by construction guys," Robert said.

"I'm not so sure," said Sandra.

"It's a joke," said Robert. "Construction guys are working on the basement of a house that's not built yet. They're horsing around. One of them writes 'no house here' in a spot that's going to be covered up. I bet there are lots of doodles we don't see. I know there are measuring marks. And he writes 'no house' because there isn't a house yet – just planks and maybe a roof. He's being silly."

"He didn't write 'no house,'" said Sandra. "He wrote 'there is no home here.'"

"Same difference," said Robert. "He's right. There wasn't."

"It's different. Why would he write that?"

"To let off stress. Maybe make a buddy laugh. This isn't sinister."

"It's awful," said Sandra. "I think it's an awful thing to write. It's not funny. It's ominous."

"Okay," said Robert. "It's an unusual choice of wording. Maybe it's an in joke. Maybe if we knew the guy who wrote it, it would make sense. Maybe the carpenter is bald, and everyone calls him Chrome Dome."

"What?" said Sandra. "That makes no sense."

"It does; people play rhyme games. It's innate. Inside jokes spawn inside jokes. It's like lingual drift. It starts with chrome dome, and then motor home, and then no place like home – then oh no, no home, and he's No Home for the rest of the week."

"I like how you ignore Occam's Razor whenever it's inconvenient," said Sandra.

"It makes perfect sense," said Robert. "You're just obstinately determined to be upset. You got scared alone in the basement, and now you're embarrassed. I'm saying, baby, it's okay. You can just not be scared. It's okay."

"Robert," said Sandra, "you are not a trained psychologist. Nor are you a construction worker."

"Did you somehow never have friends?" said Robert. "Have you honestly never had friends with in-jokes and catchphrases and..."

"Robert. I just think you're wrong."

"Well, I know you're overreacting."

"And I think you're wrong."

Later in the day, Sandra apologized.

"I'm stressed out," she said. "I'm not sleeping well."

"Oh, gosh, of course," said Robert. "Me too, actually." He was lying. His sleep was the best part of his day. Sandra was also lying. She despised sleep and the need to sleep. She worried what might happen to her late at night. Yet moments after she lay in the bed, or sat on an overstuffed chair, she went unconscious. That night, Robert thoughtfully gave her warm milk, and took extra care to close the blinds fully. When Sandra promptly dropped to sleep, he took credit. She drank warm milk at bedtime for a week, despite the summer heat. Finally she "forgot" to buy milk at the grocery store.

When she slept easily, Robert said: "I guess that milk did the trick. It just broke you out of that pattern."

Nothing in the Basement

He smiled.

"I can't believe it," said Sandra, smiling back. "Who could have guessed." She did not tell him that all week, she had dreamed about his face distorting with anger, and imagined how it would feel to have his hands wrapped around her head. She did not tell him that sometimes she saw his face distorting even when she was awake.

Chapter 27

When the plumbing bill arrived, it amounted to more than two years' worth of mortgage payments. The first time Sandra looked at the number, her eyes skipped the decimal point, and multiplied the total by a factor of one hundred. When her brain made the obvious correction, she still struggled to grasp the total.

"You didn't tell me it was this much," she said.

"Yes, I did," said Robert.

"You told me it was a lot," said Sandra.

"I did," said Robert.

"This is two semesters of college," said Sandra. "This is one fourth of a master's degree at a very good business school."

"What's done is done," said Robert. "We could hardly let the problem go. If you think about it, it's a small price to pay for getting our house back. It's not even a tenth the cost of a new house in this neighborhood."

Sandra picked at the edge of the paper. *Why are you so sanguine all of a sudden*, she wanted to say. She knew it was petty. She knew that calling Robert a hypocrite would not help. But he was a hypocrite. It seemed calculated to make her feel irrational. If she approved of spending money, he lectured. If she worried about money, he relaxed. Her better side, which she tried to indulge, insisted that no, he'd just changed his mind. He was making a peace offering, a tone-deaf one. He should be respected.

"I don't understand, is all," she conciliated. "They were only here for two days. How can two days equal two semesters?"

Robert snorted. "It's two long dangerous days for a whole team of guys who gave up a weekend and used pricey equipment. I'm sure they'd have given us an evening power-point presentation for significantly less."

Sandra knocked her cup off the table just to bang something.

"Oh no," she said. Robert was ready with a dish towel.

"I'll get it," he said. "You just stay put while I make sure I grab everything." He diligently swabbed around her bare feet.

"There you go," he said. He rested a hand on her knee.

"It's okay," he said. "We got this. We're lucky, and smart, and we have savings. What else is money for than comfort, and what is more comfortable than not having a basement full of shit? What do you say I make us some drinks and we watch a Disney movie? What do you say, princess?"

"Okay," said Sandra.

They watched *Sleeping Beauty*, and Sandra debated, as usual, which fairy she'd become. She hoped the kind one who made cake badly, but she suspected one of the others. Pompous or bitchy – what a choice.

"I've always liked the fetish aspect of Maleficent," said Robert. "All that bondage play with Prince Phillip. It's so coy. You don't see a Disney villain like that any more. These days, heroines are oppressed by the patriarchy. It's limiting. Little girls should know they have the option of being an evil queen. These days, you can identify the villainess because she's fat or neurotic."

Nothing in the Basement

"And I'm both," said Sandra. "So I guess role models count."

"Yes. We're very proud of you," said Robert. He kissed the top of her head. "And I hope you realize that you're joking."

The following day, Robert got home before Sandra, and was careful to pre-sort the mail. About half the envelopes were requests from charities; Robert opened them, found phone numbers, and called to tell them that Sandra was dead and should be removed from their mailing lists. He set aside alumni-fund bait from Sandra's college. He piled them all on a cookie sheet, and set the oven to 475 degrees. When Sandra got home, all that remained was smudgy white dust underneath some coffee grounds in the bottom of the trash can.

"Burned my toast," Robert said when asked about the smell. The dogs avoided the kitchen. Increasingly, they spent their days on the upper floor.

The emptiness beneath the house had no thoughts or motivations. When you dug a hole, you made it. A house was enclosed. The nothing frightened the dogs because it helped no one and belonged to no one.

Chapter 28

Robert and Sandra were at an outlet store, looking for slacks he could wear to a friend's daughter's wedding. The wedding was semi-formal but luau themed. Sandra's only concession to theme was a small palm tree pin, which she intended to wear with the black knit dress she wore to all weddings. She refused to spend money to accommodate kitsch.

Robert faced a different problem. How do you make a Hawaiian shirt semi-formal? Jeans were out. Khakis were out. His two pairs of suit pants were unmistakably suit pants. To make matters worse, one pair was a formal black, and made him look like a waiter. Others weren't fitting well lately, and needed the camouflage of a jacket.

"I suppose the ideal would be beaded leather leggings – buff, supple, with a parrot." He flicked through the hangers, satisfied and annoyed by the clicking sound.

"God, it doesn't matter," said Sandra. "You're her parents' friend. She doesn't even know your name. Nobody is going to be looking at you."

"I will add to a festive atmosphere," said Robert. "I am determined. Perhaps my forward thinking will presage a romantic interlude with a hula girl."

Sandra snorted.

"Laugh if you must. I will drown my sorrows in repulsive piña coladas, and I shall insist upon multiple umbrellas. If necessary, I will steal them while everyone is distracted by the cake cutting."

"Maybe I should go look at purses," said Sandra. She stayed where she was. Robert was pleased, but knew better than to say anything. He turned to another row of unsuitable off-color slacks.

His true wish was for pants that would make him seem sophisticated and in on every joke. He knew he would not find them. He would settle for pants that did not seem like him – even if they made him look like a man with a mid-life crisis. Anything was better than being taken for someone bogged down with house repairs. And if Sandra seemed miffed about the clothes, it would cover the subtle signs that she might be angry about something else. Maybe they could have a real fight – get rid of some tension. Or maybe she'd smile and play along. Relax and get champagne misty about the new couple.

"Hey – maybe once we've got the house stuff settled, we should go on vacation – recharge a little," he said.

"Great idea," said Sandra. "A big trip right when we're out of money. Let's go to Vegas and bet the mortgage."

"Well, madam peevish," said Robert knowing immediately but not in time that it was <u>not</u> a funny, teasing thing to say. "I was thinking more along the lines of a bed and breakfast in Virginia. Nearby, romantic. Take a Friday off."

"Great," said Sandra. She barely opened her mouth. "Civil War battlefields."

"There were Revolutionary battles as well," said Robert. "You could bring a book."

"Why don't you go, and I'll stay and read at home?"

"Okay," said Robert.

Chapter 29

It was at this point that the house truly began to work on Robert. He didn't notice a difference, nor did Sandra. He was more easily tired. His morning sit-ups plateaued.

"You know, I think I am going to take that trip," said Robert.

"Oh," said Sandra. She sat down.

"No –" said Robert. "It's not... I was really inspired by what you did with the basement," he said. "Really. Using your money when you needed it. I think sometimes I worry too much about the future. I'll make up the savings. I'm not buying a business in a South American country. It's maybe a few hundred dollars for a weekend I <u>need</u>. I can spare it. I'm still safe. I'd just like to take a vacation I can look back on, that I can think of when I think of this time."

"Are you seriously holding the basement against me?" said Sandra.

"<u>No</u>," said Robert. "And you're still invited."

"Not really," said Sandra.

"You are."

"You don't really want me there."

"Yes I do. What are you doing?" Robert looked down at her. It made him a little angry that she was sitting and he was standing. It made him seem like he was making a power play – like he was dominating her and the conversation. There was an implied threat. Only she'd been standing up when he'd started talking. And he did not want to crouch to her level, or below her level. He didn't want to kowtow. He was an equal, damnit. He had no reason to apologize. He knew an apology might be politic, regardless, but when Sandra got like this, he was torn between wanting to rescue her and wanting to avoid reinforcing her behavior.

"You don't want me there," Sandra repeated, "and I don't want to be there. Why would I go? We'd both have a better time if I didn't."

"I think I'd have a better time with you," said Robert.

"You wouldn't," said Sandra. "I'll be miserable, and you'll have to make it up to me, and it won't be a vacation, and all you'll remember afterward is how difficult I was and how I ruined everything."

"I don't think that's true," said Robert.

"It *is*," said Sandra.

"Could you not be miserable?" said Robert.

"A vacation would not be vacation for me right now," said Sandra. "Everything in my life has been disrupted, and what I want now, more than anything else, is routine. Is reassurance that things are normal and are going to be normal. I want to go to bed at a regular time. I want to work a normal work week. I want to run errands to the post office. All I would think all weekend is that the stuff I'm taking off from is piling up, and I'll still have to do all of it. It's a bad time."

She stood up. "I think you should go, though," she said. "If you think you need the time away, I think you should take it."

"I could stay," said Robert.

"But you don't want to," said Sandra.

"I do," said Robert.

Nothing in the Basement

"Oh, just go," said Sandra. "Go, and come back, and don't bring me any souvenirs for god's sake, because I will throw them away."

Chapter 30

Robert packed methodically, as usual, but had to ask Sandra's help figuring out wheroe to fit his spare shoes – also as usual. This charmed Sandra every time. There was something helplessly adorable about it. Had the rest of his packing been messy, she would not have been amused. Sandra did not want children; she wanted less a man who was a child. It was not true helplessness; Robert had once confided that before Sandra, he'd simply carried an extra bag solely for shoes, or carried no extra shoes. What got to Sandra was Robert's genuine bafflement about how to place shoes in the same receptacle as clothing and toiletry. She wondered whether he'd been told too many times not to put his shod feet on the bed or the couch. Was the idea of shoe soles and fabric subconsciously too much to bear? Ultimately, she perceived an inability to deal with irregular three-dimensional shapes. Men were supposed to be brilliant at spatial reasoning, but at least for Robert, that reasoning seemed limited. Two-dimensional planes and rectangular prisms, the occasional cylinder. If it couldn't stack and wasn't small enough to fit into another container that could stack, Robert couldn't think his way into it. Sandra flipped the shoes upside down, wiggled them until they made themselves nests, and zipped the suitcase.

It occurred to Sandra that she would not be there on the other end to pack Robert's shoes for the trip back. This fact made her feel melancholy. He would probably carry the shoes in a plastic bag, or some freebie tote. He was brilliant at securing free tote bags. He brought them back from almost every business trip. At least one contained shoes, and another might contain more free tote bags. Sandra had had to find a school charity that would accept them as book bags for low-income students, just to convince Robert to part with them. Tenderness overwhelmed her as if a small and prickly animal had run up her arms and taken residence in her chest.

It was an increasingly rare feeling. She tried to fan it, nurture it. She thought about other nice things Robert did - not grand gestures, but small peculiar pleasantries. When he used the saltshaker, he didn't use it directly. He tapped it against his wrist. His other affectations sometimes bothered Sandra, but his salt dispersing was emphatically matter-of-fact - an engineer's embrace of a controlled spray pattern.

The time apart would be good for them, she thought sternly. It was easier to remember what she liked about Robert when she wasn't faced with the stress of day-to-day picking. They were in a rut. Things had been stressful, and they'd gotten stuck in a pattern of discontent. Some breathing space, and they'd be ready to appreciate what they had together.

She blamed a lack of business trips.

They'd had to savor their time together during the honeymoon years when he'd flown around the country for conferences, and she'd been back and forth to the Burbank office. She'd never bought into the stories about couples driving each other crazy when one retired. That seemed like the sort of thing that would only happen to dull people who didn't like each other. But maybe those people were right.

Nothing in the Basement

Maybe she and Robert just spent too much time together. Or maybe she and Robert were very wrong; which would at least be nice to know.

"Have a good time," she said, kissing his cheek. "I mean it about no souvenirs.

"Should I call at night?" he said. She thought.

"No," she said. "Have a real vacation. I really want to miss you. Don't even leave your phone on. Otherwise, you know, work..."

"Yeah, work," he said. "Okay. I left the number for the hotel, if you need me." He kissed her again. "I love you."

She waved until his car turned at the end of the street.

When Robert arrived at the bed and breakfast and opened his suitcase, he released some of the emptiness that he'd carried from the house. It sank into low spaces and began to fester. The new bride next door began to think she'd chosen the wrong design for her wedding band. She dreaded what people might think of her for the rest of her life, and what she'd think looking at her hand with that ring. At breakfast, there was no coffee; mold had coated the coffee maker. Robert didn't notice. He slept late.

Chapter 31

Sandra did not advertise that Robert had left town. She had assumed in advance that it would require excuses, and that she might be deluged with visitors determined to keep her from getting lonely. But in fact, nobody noticed. The entire weekend, no one called. This was deflating, but it was also a relief, but it was also deflating. She wanted someone to be concerned. She wanted to trigger a strong feeling one way or the other – somebody who would tell her she was a fool, and that Robert was great and should be cut more slack. Somebody who would tell her that Robert was a beast and she was a fool to stay. Then she could say angrily that she loved him very much or say angrily that she was miserable and overlooked. Then she would know what she felt.

She called her mother and asked her to lunch. Then she panicked. Then she felt clever. Her mother both liked Robert and was firmly on Sandra's side. And her mother certainly couldn't guilt trip her for a bad marriage. Best of all, if her mother chose to express an opinion in front of Robert, it would seem like the usual presumptuous tactlessness - not something that had come from Sandra. Ace.

"This gourmet ice cream drives me crazy," said her mother. "I love it, but it drives me crazy. Saffron peach. Rice melon. Remember the days of just chocolate and vanilla, strawberry if you were lucky? Awful. Limiting. But now, all these choices. You always feel like you made the wrong decision. You find one you like and stick to it, and you feel boring. You switch every time and you think, ugh, why didn't I just get one I knew I liked? Before, you could have a favorite. Maybe you didn't like it that much, and maybe it was chalky, but it was a favorite. Now it's impossible. And they want me to know what farm the cow lives on. God forbid it's even a real cow and not rice. I'm trying to sit down and have a conversation with my daughter. They want me to scan a code and look at live video of the cow. And what are they getting? Ad revenue."

"Nobody is doing that," said Sandra. "Who is doing that?"

"They should give me a radio show," said her mother. "Not TV. I never want to wear makeup again. But radio, I'd be famous."

Her mother ordered vanilla ice cream.

"Robert and I are having problems," said Sandra.

"Dramatic," said her mother. "I like it."

"I'm serious," said Sandra.

"I know," said her mother. "I just hoped you weren't. Has he decided he wants kids? That happens."

"No," said Sandra. "No large change in philosophy. No affairs. Money trouble, I guess, but not really."

"I don't know," her mother said. "That stuff is more stressful than most people think. Worrying over money, being tired and not sleeping. This is why senior citizens carefully schedule meals and go to sleep at 9. We know."

"I think it's more serious than that," said Sandra. "I mean, we're fighting a little about stupid things, but I'm sure that's temporary. But I don't think I'm in love with him. I'm worried that I wasn't ever in love with him. We get along, and he's my friend, but I'm not crazy about him, you know? I don't shiver when he walks into a room. Did I used to? Not really, but I'm sure it was more than now."

"Oh, honey," said her mother. "This sounds like a midlife crisis. Like your father's midlife crisis, specifically. He needed to puff himself up, feel like he was attractive to younger women. It mostly blew over when he got a new haircut. Hair matters. Never doubt it."

"That's the thing," said Sandra. "I'm perfectly happy with my life, although now that you mention it, not with my hair. I don't really know. I feel like I should be feeling something, which makes me sound like a teenager obsessed with Sylvia Plath. I look at Robert, and on the one hand, I recognize him as a person who I like. On the other hand, it's like looking at a computer simulation. A zombie Robert, who looks and talks like my husband, but I could shoot him in the head."

"Well," said Sandra's mother, "I think the main thing is not to buy a gun. And I'm relieved to hear you're not happy with your hair, because I've tried not to say anything, but it's frumpy. It makes me feel old, and not in the good way. I know I'm supposed to be liberated now and not worry about these things, but even lesbians recognize the defining qualities of a haircut. Perhaps lesbians most of all. We practically signal with them. And you are signaling frumpy. You are signaling defeated. We have to get you to a good stylist immediately. My treat."

Sandra considered the proposition. A new haircut meant new maintenance – perhaps new hair products. The idea was exhausting. She worried that a haircut *would* send a signal: an emergency beacon. Maybe Robert would come back and think she got him out of the way in order to change her hair – an odd combative move. Part of her knew this train of thought made very little sense. The train, however, did not stop.

"Maybe next week?" said Sandra.

"Nothing doing," said her mother, who snapped for the check the way people did in movies. It did not work. However, the waiter came by to check on them a few minutes later, and before Sandra knew it, the bill had been paid and she was sitting in front of a large mirror while a butch yet elfin woman asked her how she wanted to manifest her power.

"With my hair?" said Sandra.

"Yes – but with *whose* hair?" asked the stylist.

"My concept," said Sandra's mother, "is a frontier sheriff. Tough, no nonsense, but cultured – a tough-as-nails sharpshooter who tries to set a civilized example for the roughnecks."

"I know exactly what you mean," said the stylist. "I can do it."

And she did.

When it was done, Sandra looked younger without looking like she was trying to look young. She found herself focusing on her eyes instead of her mouth. She couldn't tell whether that was a good thing. Would people pay more or less attention to what she was saying? She suspected she would look, at the very least, like she meant whatever it was she said. She also looked less feminine, less homey. No one would suspect her of living in the suburbs; no one would ask her to bake cookies. She wasn't sure she wanted to be this fighter lady. Maybe sparkly clips in the front? She knew a haircut always took her a few days to adjust. It made her feel panicked, and little weepy.

Nothing in the Basement

"Wow," said Sandra. "I look very forceful. I think it looks good – I mean, I like what it does for my chin. But I look very forceful."

"You look like yourself, darling," said her mom.

Chapter 32

Robert had always thought of himself as a man who would have enlisted to fight for the Union army. Most of the Civil War buffs liked the romance of the Confederacy – the doomed fight for a way of life, even a repellant one. The stuff of poetry. The gallant pike charges. Even Pickett's charge. It was the elegance of old aristocracy and the wild daring of cowboys. Robert was a Union man. He'd never held to aristocracy, or irregulars. He protected the capitol, and he did it in a regimented way, with shoes, railroads, and interchangeable rifle parts. If there weren't as many great eccentrics on the Union side – no Hood's Texas Brigade, no lemon-eating Stonewall Jackson – maybe it was because the Union didn't need personality cults. The eccentric leaders hadn't needed deification because they hadn't lost.

Nevertheless, Robert called the battle site Manassas instead of Bull Run, even in his head. It seemed more respectful to the people who lived there. He spent the day wandering across the rolling fields, reapplying sun block at regular intervals. It didn't give him the same satisfaction he expected. Normally, he felt some of the same solemn peace he felt at large cemeteries, and monuments to fallen leaders. Normally, he looked at the hills and trees and felt how startling it must have been to have your house commandeered, and shortly thereafter, to witness a loud and brutal battle which left bodies thick on the ground. He looked at a tree, and it was more than a tree. It was a tree incorporated with nutrients from the blood of fallen soldiers. The tree had been the last vision of a man dying for deeply held principles, baffled that his country had deserted him.

Robert should have lapsed into melancholy. Thoughts of war made Sandra sad, not unusual in the general population. Instead, Robert quarreled with absent people – people who did not exist. The pleasures of a thirty year hobby deserted him entirely. He felt only simmering rage as the day went on. He should have left the battlefield and found something else – something genuinely relaxing. He stayed through sheer stubbornness.

"What a fucking waste," he thought. Fucking fields. The fields were, for the Union, only a point on a line. The Confederates fought for their home – desperate to repulse an invading army. Only the Union wasn't invading, goddamnit. The Confederacy had no right to secede. It was cheating. It was poor sportsmanship.

Robert didn't just follow the laws he agreed with. He went the speed limit like everyone else. Buying a helicopter didn't mean you didn't have to pay the taxes for roads. Romanticize cheating all you like. The law will come after you, and they will be right to do so. Robert had had friends in college who protested and engaged in acts of civil disobedience. When cops arrested them, they were livid. He did not sympathize. A legal system that needed change was better than anarchy. Ask anyone who'd lived in a country without a government: *any* regime was better than no regime.

He marched along Chinn Ridge. What the hell kind of strategy was the South using, long term? Kill enough Union men – *law* men – and figure the rest will give up? How was the end not inevitable? Why drag it out? Why bring on so much death? Why complain when the winning side, the side of law, was actually accommodating? Sure, the Union burned down some towns, but they were towns full of goddamn terrorists. He thought of how Longstreet's tactical command had won the day for the Confederates – had put them in a position to attack Washington. After the South lost, a generation of bitter men had blamed it on Longstreet, simply because he had the audacity to be a gracious loser. When he surrendered, he really surrendered. He went back to work for the U.S. Government, keeping peace and protecting ex-slaves. It probably helped that he was a straightforward Tennessee man, instead of one of the damn courtly Virginians.

Robert stood on Stone Bridge and looked at the disgusting tourists. He was overwhelmed with a desire to get out of Virginia, monument to sore-loserdom. However, he had paid for another two nights of bed and breakfast. He drove around until he found a restaurant named after a North Atlantic state. He ordered something large and steak-based. He spent the rest of the day drinking ale and eating various potatoes while working his way through a Regency-period Romance novel loaned to him by his waitress. When the restaurant closed, she kindly dropped him off. Although he was very drunk, he was smart enough to recognize it as kindness rather than a sexual advance.

The following day, Robert suffered through an ice cream social and a quilting exhibit. He was very hung over. He tried to call Sandra, but he'd forgotten both his cell phone charger and her number.

Chapter 33

During Robert's absence, Sandra avoided going into the basement. She didn't notice until Sunday, when she dripped chocolate ice cream onto her blouse and desperately scrubbed it at the kitchen sink instead of going to the laundry room.

"This is ridiculous," she thought. "There is nothing down there." It took her another hour and a cup of chamomile tea to get up the nerve to confirm.

"Hello?" she called down the stairs, feeling foolish. She flipped on the basement light. Everything looked normal. Carpet-less, but normal. A faint odor of wafting sewage remained, but it was so faint that Sandra couldn't be sure she wasn't imagining it.

"Hello?" she said again. Her heart was pounding. She was less afraid of being attacked than of seeing something horrible; she'd always felt she would make a dignified and feisty murder victim, but horror movies gave her nightmares. She thumped a hand onto the banister, closed her eyes, and descended.

When she reached the bottom of the stairs, she tried to take another step down. And felt shock as her foot made contact with floor inches earlier than she'd expected.

"Aa!" she said. Just "aa." In an empty house. Not too embarrassing.

Nothing in the Basement

"Motherfucker!" she added, for good measure. She opened her eyes. The south wall was blank. The west wall was blank. She turned. Her stomach sunk.

Rusty dirty red smeared the wall under the stairs. Streaks radiated like scrabbling handprints. A head-sized blotch floated just above the missing baseboard.

Sandra ran upstairs and dialed the only number she could think of.

"Hello?" said the sister at the forensic cleaners. In the background, Sandra could hear furniture moving.

"Hi," said Sandra, proud of the evenness of her voice. "This is Sandra Brown, and I wondered..."

"Oh, Jeez," said the sister, "we still haven't gotten those photos back to you. I'm sorry. I was supposed to call."

"It's okay," said Sandra.

"We are working on them," said the sister. "I promise. Nothing missing, or broken, or ineffective. We got hit by a rush of emergency jobs, and you know my brother. Big hero. Figured it was priority to help desperate people get back on their feet. We're at a house right now – some joker at school fed this thirteen-year-old kid some baloney about Satanic rituals and immortality."

"Baloney?" said Sandra. She felt as though she was standing next to herself. Her eyes never left the basement door.

"Not literal baloney," said the sister. "Metaphorical baloney. Hogwash, if you will. So the kid drew a pentagram in his bedroom and butchered the family cat. It's insane. I like to think he was led astray and will straighten out after this – straight-A student. It's hard not to fit in. At least he was smart enough not to check his own immortality afterward."

Nothing in the Basement

"I was a pretty crazy teenager," Sandra said. She had never killed a cat. She had made herself sick through a misinformed granola-only diet. Was the door moving?

"Listen," said Sandra, edging closer to the wall, "don't worry about the pictures. I mean, worry about them, but take your time. But I was wondering - there are red streaks on the wall?"

"Ohhhh," said the sister. She exhaled. Sandra got the impression that she was not a person who smoked, but had in the past. "Yeah. That happens sometimes. Kind of a rust color, but bright?"

"<u>Yes</u>," said Sandra.

"Mmmhmm," said the sister. "That's bacteria that likes to gobble up the microscopic leftovers of human waste. I wouldn't worry about it; it's ugly as sin, but it won't give you respiratory problems. If you get black stuff, call someone. But the red stuff will die off once it starves. Wipe the wall down with vinegar; it'll come right off. It might come back a few times, but that just means it's nibbling, trying to finish the job. If you really get tired of looking at it, KILZ the fucker. Forty bucks."

"You think it's helping?" said Sandra.

"Yeah. In a totally self-interested way." In the background, Sandra heard a thump, and some cursing from the stocky cousin.

"Listen," said the sister, "I've got to get back to work before these knuckleheads tear the place up. Is there anything else I can help you with?"

"Well," said Sandra, "does this mean anything to you - There Is No Home Here?"

"That's fuckin' creepy," said the sister.

Nothing in the Basement

"I pulled out a board in the basement, and that's what was written underneath."

"Written?" said the sister. "Like, burned into the wood?"

"No," said Sandra. "Just written in pencil."

"Oh." The sister relaxed again. "Probably just a joke, then. You know – construction workers."

"I guess," said Sandra.

"I really have to go," said the sister. "Are you going to be okay?"

"Yeah," said Sandra. "Yes."

"You have a good afternoon," said the sister. "Call back if there's anything else. I mean it."

"Thanks," said Sandra. She held the phone long after the line went dead.

Chapter 34

When Robert got home, the dogs didn't welcome him. They didn't bark at him either. They just didn't care.

"Say," said Robert. "It looks like you finally learned to stop jumping on people, huh?"

He was disappointed.

Sandra wasn't home. He welcomed her back in the evening when she came through the door with bags of groceries.

"You're back early," said Sandra.

"Yep," said Robert. "You pickling something?"

"No," said Sandra. She set the vinegar bottles in a neat line across the counter.

"How was your trip?" she asked, not looking at him.

"Oh," he said. "Kind of boring. I saw some quilts you'd have liked. Lots of sage green like you like."

"How nice," said Sandra.

"The bed and breakfast was supposedly haunted, but the ghost never showed. Two ghosts, actually. One is supposed to be a young woman who looks out a window and waits for her husband to come home from the war. The other is this old man who tells stories and asks whether you have whiskey. Never showed." He walked around the kitchen island. "Hey," he said. "Come 'ere." He wrapped his arms around Sandra. She relaxed.

"I missed you," she said.

Nothing in the Basement

"I missed you, too," said Robert. "I like your hair."

They spent the afternoon killing time in a pleasant way – watched some recorded TV shows, played a few rounds of Boggle. Sandra baked chocolate chip cookies from a tube, worse tasting but more decadent than cookies made from scratch. They went to bed early and had leisurely sex - pleasurable for both of them. And they were both relieved when, in the morning, they got into separate cars and drove to work in opposite directions.

The emptiness beneath the house had no thoughts or motivations. It angered the dogs. When you dug a hole, you made it. The nothing frightened the dogs because it helped no one and belonged to no one.

Chapter 35

The following week, during another run of ninety-degree temperatures, the air conditioner broke again. A handyman charged them an expert's hourly rate to replace a fuse and tell them that the filter should be changed.

"When was the last time you replaced this?" said the handyman.

"I don't know," said Robert. "A year? Year and a half?"

"Yeah," said the handyman, hitching up his belt. "You got to replace these every three months, especially with pets in the home. Otherwise, things get clogged. The motor has to work hard, it blows a fuse. You understand what I'm saying?"

"Yep," said Robert.

"You have to replace the filter. Every three months," said the handyman.

"Okay," said Robert.

"Otherwise, I'm going to be out here. You understand?"

"Yep," said Robert. He passed the relevant information to Sandra, who turned on him immediately.

"You mean you haven't been replacing the filter?" she accused.

"Hey – you haven't replaced it either," said Robert. "How is this my fault?"

"Because it's your *job*," said Sandra.

Nothing in the Basement

"Well, obviously, I didn't know that," said Robert, matching her volume. "And that's why I didn't do it. You need to calm down."

"I am calm," yelled Sandra. "I just want you to admit that this went down on your watch, and promise it won't happen again."

"I'm not going to do anything until you stop yelling at me," yelled Robert.

"You stop yelling at me," yelled Sandra. "I am not yelling."

"Jesus," said Robert. "Why are you so concerned with blame all the time? Are you really so insecure that you can't handle thinking that somewhere you might have made a mistake? We both forgot!"

"I did not forget!" Sandra yelled. "I remembered! I just thought I didn't have to worry about it! I thought I could trust you to be an adult! I thought you wouldn't want me to nag you! Is that what you want? Should I make you a schedule?"

"You never told me once!" shouted Robert. "If that's your version of not nagging, that is some secretive bullshit! I would have been happy to go to the hardware store! I like to go to the hardware store! Stop trying to blame me!"

"I am not crazy!" yelled Sandra. "My actions follow other actions. You come in here, mad because you got told off by some handyman, and you pick a fight with me to blow off steam! I'm! Not! Interested!"

"That is not what happened!" shouted Robert.

"I am not crazy!" yelled Sandra.

Conversations went on like this for the next month. Not every conversation, but at least two a week. Enough that the other conversations made them jumpy. One or the other would start to relax – think things were over. Then another fight started. Often, they had trouble knowing what the fights were about, which made it hard to avoid them or apologize afterward. Each began to think of the other as moody. They tried to spend more time at home, to buffer the fights with memories of cozy domesticity. They had an easier time getting along when friends were present, since each could be sure of backup. At the same time, they avoided seeing friends together, out of a fear that a fight would break out unstoppably, mysteriously.

The weather got cooler, and then hot again.

It made no difference.

Chapter 36

Pilgrim started licking himself like a cat, and chewing on his paws until he pulled the hair out. Sandra tried putting bitter oil on his feet, but that didn't stop him. She bought him new chew toys. Eventually, she put him in a plastic cone, the kind you give animals to stop them from pulling out stitches. The sight depressed her, so she started feeding him half tablets of old Prozac.

"I know why you're nervous," she thought. "I can't help it."

She started taking the other Prozac half. She had enough to last a few weeks; after that, she'd have to get a prescription. Or find a teenager. You could buy things from teenagers. A middle-aged woman lurking around a high school would not attract the same attention as a middle-aged man. This thought precipitated an internal women's studies war about the assumption that women were nurturers unable to disrupt the status quo.

Robert auditioned for, and got into, a community theater group. Popcorn dramas. His height made him a natural pantomime villain. He embellished his monologues. "Forsooth!" he liked to say, and: "Unhand me, ruffian!" Few cast members were serious actors. The honorariums mostly covered beer money. It felt like a geeky bowling league. Robert would drop a Monty Python reference, and he'd have a new set of drinking buddies.

Nothing in the Basement

It was a good excuse not to go home.

Most of his friends were permanent or temporary single folk filling up time. He told them he was a married bachelor, and they were amused; no one asked follow-up questions.

Robert's best quality as a performer was his generosity with the spotlight. Even in a top hat, eye patch, handlebar mustache, and high-collared cape, he could vanish into the background. When he stepped forward and spoke, it was like a magic trick. The lead actress often forgot he shared scenes, until he grabbed her arm. No matter how many times they rehearsed, she authentically gasped in shock.

"It's amazing," said the lead actor. "In the scene where we're hunting him down, I truly don't see him. I come on stage to pretend to search, but I really have to search! And he's standing right there!"

"I'm telling you," laughed the lead actress, "it's like the devil suddenly appears out of Hell, and you think 'hello! Where did you come from? Oh, Hell? Oh hell.'"

"That's giving me ideas," said the director. "It's been too long since we've had a good devil play. If we started rehearsal right after this one, we'd be in time for Halloween."

"Devil Robert!" cheered the cast.

"Ooga Booga," said Robert.

"You're all getting carried away," said the stage manager. "A guy who can disappear when he walks across stage? A guy who looks good in black? A guy who scares the bejesus out of you when you're not sure of your next line? That's no devil. That's a stage manager!"

"Stage Manager El Diablo!" cheered the cast.

Chapter 37

How could you talk to someone about a marriage in trouble, Sandra wondered. The very idea was terrifying. It was easy to say you were leaving; hard to say you were staying but unhappy. It was supposed to be the braver choice, but you looked like an idiot. If things were as bad as you said, you were a dishrag – a woman with no internal strength, and no insight. Maybe things weren't so bad. Maybe you were an emotionally unsophisticated failure, terminally unhappy.

Let anyone know, and they might call you on a cheerful day, ask "how are you feeling? Are you all right?" And you could say "I'm fine – I'm feeling great, actually," and look like a melodramatic liar, a Chicken Little crying wolf. Or you could say, "well, I'm okay, but things are still rough," and validate their worry. Answer all their follow-up questions and hang up mired and miserable.

And what about the betrayal? You can't go to someone who only knows you, or they'll hate him. It has to be someone who knows both of you, who knows why you're staying. And then you have to worry that a look of sympathy will give it away the next time you're all in a room together. Or the friend will stop coming over, because it's too tense. Or they come over and you can't relax. You feel like you're performing. *Robert finds out and is angry that I've given away his secrets. Our secrets. Talking out of school.*

Nothing in the Basement

Fighting in front of the children.

It was hard for Sandra to know who knew. People seemed relieved when she said she was tired or overworked. Maybe they were glad she let her guard down with them (they thought). Or it might mean they worried and an alternate possibility comforted them. Or they might feel relief that she wasn't dragging out dirty linen.

Sandra's photos had finally been returned, clean and neatly stacked. She set up a scrap-booking station in her office, and spent a few hours a night pasting pictures onto acid-free paper and slipping them into plastic sleeves. At first, it was an excuse to say she was working. So busy she couldn't see anyone –the work explained her exhaustion. Soon enough she looked forward to it.

She let the dogs curl around her feet. She found a television channel with endless reruns of *Golden Girls*. She wasn't much of an artist, but she had read enough magazines and Power Point presentations to have a firm grasp of layout. She left room on the page for blocks of text. She used dates as subheads. She wrote detailed captions:

"7th Grade Awards Ceremony. Sandra wins good citizenship award – like everyone else in the class. Even Billy Matthews, class clown and 10th grade dropout. Afterward, a special trip for Sandra and Dad: Coca Cola at the bar of the Palace Hotel. Miss Alice Grumley (Social Studies teacher) presiding."

While Sandra completed a page, she felt firm satisfaction. Maybe it was a stupid victory. Maybe no one would ever look at her scrapbook. If they did, they would see her life, laid out, in order, with the ugly parts carefully removed. On maudlin days, she felt she was preparing for her own death.

Nothing in the Basement

"That's right," she would think. "I am a pharaoh building my pyramid."

On happier days, she was making a hope chest for a hazy future when she would lay everything out for an appreciative audience.

Chapter 38

On a Friday night after dinner, Robert walked outside to discover that all four of his tires were flat. He looked up and down the street. No other cars had been hit. Closer examination turned up a puzzling lack of the usual accessories to teenage mischief. His car windows remained unbroken. Eggs did not spatter the paint. No beer cans littered the road. His windshield wipers worked perfectly.

Robert walked back inside with black, sooty hands. Sandra stared at him while he washed his hands at the sink.

"What happened?" she said.

"Oh, somebody let the air out of my tires," said Robert. "I couldn't find a spot where they sliced them, so I guess they deflated them, and then put the valve caps back on. In broad daylight."

"That's crazy," said Sandra.

"Yeah," said Robert. "This is supposed to be a good neighborhood. I guess we should clear out the garage so this kind of stuff doesn't happen."

"I can't believe it," said Sandra.

"So, anyway, can I borrow your car?" said Robert.

"I'd rather you didn't," said Sandra.

"Are you going to use it for anything?" said Robert.

"I don't know," said Sandra.

"Do you think I'm going to wreck it?" said Robert.

"No," said Sandra.

Nothing in the Basement

"What are you going to use it for?" said Robert.

"I don't know," said Sandra. "Maybe nothing. I don't know."

"Well, I definitely need a car, and I definitely need to use it to get to rehearsal, so can I use it?"

"Why don't you take your motorcycle?" said Sandra. "I mean, you have two vehicles. It's a nice night. Everyone will think it's really cool. Have they seen the motorcycle?"

"Sandra, I'm not running an errand for milk," said Robert. "I'm not going to a friend's house. I'm going to rehearsal, which is in a hard-up church in a shitty neighborhood. I might as well hang out a sign for thieves. I could get jumped at a stop sign, for chrissakes."

"I don't think you should go at all, if it's that dangerous," said Sandra. "I don't like the idea of a car there, either."

"Do you want to drop me off?" said Robert. "If you don't want to loan me the car, you can drop me off. It's maybe twenty minutes away. I could get a ride home from somebody."

"Could they pick you up now?"

"No, Sandra," said Robert. "No, they couldn't, because they are all already on their way to rehearsal. Instead of being able to ask everyone at once, 'hey guys, anybody want to give me a ride,' I would have to make phone calls to phones that not everyone answers. Let's go if we're going to go."

"What if nobody gives you a ride home?" said Sandra.

"Then I'll give you a call," said Robert.

"And wait outside in that bad neighborhood?" said Sandra.

"I'll give you a call before rehearsal even ends. I'll let you know in plenty of time."

Nothing in the Basement

"So I could wait outside in that bad neighborhood?" said Sandra.

"It's not some murder ghetto, Sandra," said Robert. "Nobody is going to knife you. You're not going to be raped."

"So it's safe for me, but not for the motorcycle," said Sandra.

"Jesus Christ," said Robert. "If you don't want to take me, then loan me the car. You're not even planning to go out. You don't even know why you're saying no. You're just saying no."

"It's my car!" said Sandra. "You asked me if you could borrow it, and I said no! It's not unreasonable. You don't know my plans. I don't see why we're even having this conversation!"

"What are your plans," said Robert.

"No," said Sandra.

"What are your plans," said Robert.

"No," said Sandra.

"Is it a secret?" said Robert.

"No," said Sandra.

"Jesus," said Robert. "Why are you being such a selfish bitch?"

Sandra spun around and stomped off.

"Where are you going?" yelled Robert.

Sandra stomped back; stuck some wadded toilet paper under his nose.

"You're bleeding," she said, angrily.

"Shit," swore Robert. As a child, he'd suffered constant nosebleeds – whenever he'd been angry or frustrated, his nose had become a blood spigot. He used to tell people his face was bloody from a fist fight. It hadn't happened in twenty years or more. Then again, he couldn't remember the last time he'd been so angry.

"I really can't drive a motorcycle one-handed, Sandra," said Robert.

"I think in light of all this, you should maybe stay home, don't you think?" said Sandra. "I'm not sure I like being here alone if your car was attacked."

"You're just making up excuses now," said Robert. He shifted the tissue. "If that was a genuine issue, you'd have mentioned it before. I am going to go out front, and I am going to sit on your car until rehearsal is over or you decide to come out and give me the keys. And I really hope – I *really hope* – you are a person who will do that. I really hope you are."

Robert sat outside for thirty minutes, fuming. It was clear at that point that Sandra wasn't going to come out. But he was damned if he was going back inside. He was damned if he'd give her the satisfaction. He wished he'd thought to grab a book. He couldn't think of anything but how mad he was.

And his damn nose wouldn't stop bleeding. The tissue disintegrated. Blood started wicking into his shirt cuff. Eventually, he dropped his hand, and let the gore flow onto his shirt.

"Take that," he thought. He liked the idea that the blood would horrify Sandra. She'd insist that he come back inside to clean up. Perhaps he would refuse. He also liked the idea that Sandra, still mad, would throw her keys out the window. He'd show up to rehearsal covered in blood, and everyone would pity him and think he was cool. He started to feel chilly.

"Finally, cool weather," he thought.

Nothing in the Basement

Sandra came out of the house. She stood on the front stoop and looked at him. She went back into the house. She returned a few minutes later, her purse jammed with magazines. She shoved an old towel into Robert's hands, and guided him to the passenger seat.

"Okay," burbled Robert. The blood on his lips formed tiny, silly bubbles. "Get on the highway, northbound..."

"We're not going to rehearsal," said Sandra, reversing with quick precision. "I'm taking you to the hospital."

Almost ten minutes after walking into the emergency room, Robert collapsed. He was mid-sentence, arguing with Sandra, reaching for his wallet so that he'd have his insurance card handy when they reached the front of the line. Then he was on the floor. Unconscious. His shirt, and half of the towel, were a slick murky red.

Chapter 39

Robert woke up alone in a hospital room. There were no windows. He couldn't see a clock. His arm itched. The IV running into his arm was blood-colored. The bag it came from was bloody, and the bandage that held it in place was also bloody. He didn't feel frightened. He told himself he didn't feel frightened. He was, however, concerned. In the interest of more comprehensive information, he pressed the emergency call button over and over again.

A nurse arrived and asked about his pain level. She looked at the IV bag. She wrote on a clipboard and disappeared. Nurses were always friendly and sexy in the movies. Especially in war movies. Movie characters generally were friendly and sexy, unless they wore monster makeup - nurses in particular. Watching movies as a kid, he'd wondered why people were scared of hospitals. He'd guessed it was a smell issue. Movie nurses laughed at your jokes and played cards with you, and got teary when you left even though they were glad you were well. Movie doctors were more of a crapshoot. Nurses, though. It was amazing, when you thought about it. Nurses in war zones had so much time to play cards and listen to jokes. Perhaps they did it out of respect for the purple hearts.

Robert's nurse hadn't been friendly or sexy. Maybe it was the scrubs. Maybe it was the hospital cafeteria. He remembered that his mother used to finish things if he didn't eat them. He wondered whether nurses had the same impulse for patients. That would get to you pretty quickly. He got the impression that his nurse was low income. He didn't know whether he was jumping to conclusions. Scrubs were, well, scrubby. Scrubs made nurses look homeless.

Robert wondered whether the nurse had in fact been a nurse. A patient might wander the halls and ask questions out of boredom or mental distress. The nurse had never identified herself as a nurse; she had merely behaved in a way that anyone who watched modern television could replicate. Robert hadn't thought to ask for qualifications. This not-necessarily-a-nurse had shown up after he pressed a button. It could be coincidence. The button might not even connect. When had a flight attendant ever arrived so promptly? And where was Robert? A hospital, certainly. Who was his primary caregiver? Where was his personal doctor? Where was Sandra? Robert had to look out for himself. Hadn't he heard news stories? A tangle of overlapping doctors could lead to wrong prescriptions, to opportunistic diseases and unnecessary complications? Robert needed to settle the nurse business. He pressed the emergency call button again.

The nurse walked in again. She looked mad, or tired. Robert had trouble understanding her face. He was pretty sure she was a nurse.

"Are you all right?" said the nurse. "Do you need the bathroom?"

"What time is it?" said Robert. "Can I talk to a doctor?"

Sandra walked in, and the nurse left. Sandra looked pale. Her hair was messy. She sat on the edge of the bed and put a hand on his hand.

"How are you doing?" she asked.

Nothing in the Basement

"Where were you?" said Robert.

"Coffee," said Sandra, raising a paper cup and jiggling it. "I've been awake a long time. I wanted to be here when you woke up."

"What's going on?" said Robert.

"I know this sounds ominous," said Sandra, "but the doctor's supposed to be back in another few hours, and I'd rather let her talk to you."

"Nice suspense," said Robert. Sandra looked down.

"You're okay," she said. "I asked a lot of questions, and everything sounds very manageable. I mean, if this hasn't been a problem for you before now, it must not be very serious. I'm acting like a coward, but I think that if I say anything you're not going to believe me and you're going to get frustrated and ask a lot of questions I can't answer. That's why I'm not saying anything – not because I can't handle telling you you're going to die, or that you need surgery, or whatever. Just because it's weird."

"Am I going to die?" said Robert.

"No," said Sandra.

"Am I going to need surgery?" said Robert.

"No," said Sandra. "Just ongoing preventative care."

"This is like being on a really tedious game show," said Robert. "Just tell me what's going on. I'm not going to call you a liar and attack you with questions."

"I didn't say you'd think I was a liar," said Sandra.

"You did," said Robert. "You said I wouldn't believe you."

"Well, that's not the same thing as saying you'll think I'm a liar," said Sandra.

"How – never mind," said Robert. "What –"

"You could think I'm stupid," said Sandra. "You could... I have had way too much coffee at this point. I have to sleep."

Nothing in the Basement

"You can't sleep," said Robert. "You've had too much coffee."

"I have had too much coffee!" said Sandra. She rubbed her thumb along his knuckles.

"You have hemophilia," said Sandra.

"That's ridiculous," said Robert.

"You see?" said Sandra. She sipped her coffee triumphantly.

Chapter 40

Robert watched TV, which helped him keep track of the time. He had trouble following the plots. He couldn't tell whether this meant they were inane and convoluted, or if it was psychopharmeceuticals. Maybe he kept falling asleep and waking up without noticing. Sandra was no help; she'd dropped into an uncomfortable snooze, curled in an armchair. A nurse – a different nurse – came in and took down Robert's blood bag. She left a large and a small bag of clear liquid.

Robert's doctor was a petite Indian woman. Possibly she was not Robert's doctor, but the hospital's specialist, or the generalist on ward, or a resident. She was doctor somebody. She spoke in a clipped accent as she explained, all in a rush, that he had Hemophilia Type A, and that his blood had limited amounts of an important clotting factor, and that he had been infused with both a dose of this clotting factor and donated sterilized blood. As soon as he was feeling up to it, she believed he was safe to go home. The hospital would be happy to give him a complete list of local specialists. There were exactly two.

"This is all interesting," said Robert, "and I'm not trying to be difficult. But I don't have hemophilia."

"Oh, really?" said the doctor. "You simply began bleeding spontaneously, and your blood did not clot, and our blood tests told us you had hemophilia, and you recovered when we injected clotting factor eight?"

"I'm not trying to tread on your territory," said Robert, "but no. I do not have hemophilia."

"Are you a doctor?" said the doctor.

"No," said Robert.

"Have you been to medical school?" said the doctor.

"No," said Robert. "But I have read a lot about Rasputin, and Queen Victoria, and European history, and it's my understanding that hemophilia is genetic."

"It is," said the doctor. "You inherited it from your mother."

"No," said Robert. He smiled because he was reasonable and good-humored. He had faced down protesters outside his office. He had worked with both politicians and social scientists. "No one in my family is a hemophiliac," he said.

"They are all carriers, then," said the doctor. "The genetic mutation is carried on the X chromosome, and –"

"The odds against that are extraordinary," said Robert.

"As are the odds for human life," said the doctor. "Perhaps it is a miracle."

She did not look as though she believed it was a miracle.

"Or perhaps your gene mutated, and you have introduced a special new genetic line of Hemophilia A. Congratulations."

"You can develop hemophilia as an adult?" said Robert.

"No," said the doctor. "Your gene mutated in the womb, if that is what happened."

"But I didn't have hemophilia yesterday," said Robert.

"You did," said the doctor. "You have had it since birth."

Robert wished he could pace, or crumple something. "I used to play hockey," he explained, "and –"

"Oh – you cannot play hockey any longer," said the

118

doctor. "You must not participate in any contact sports."

"No," said Robert, grinding his teeth. "Listen. I used to play hockey. I used to get beaten up by bullies. I have given blood on multiple occasions..."

"You must not give blood," said the doctor. "It is not safe for you or for..."

"If I had hemophilia," said Robert, "how could I possibly go through all that and not notice?"

He started laughing, and he wasn't sure why.

"Don't you think," he said.

The doctor handed him some leaflets and snapped her folder shut. "I deal in facts," she said, "not speculations. You are a hemophiliac, and that is a fact, and we have tested it. And if you are a hemophiliac, which you are, you were born a hemophiliac and have always been a hemophiliac. You may find it very funny, but I do not find it funny. I do not find it funny to argue about facts. I suggest you discuss this matter with a psychiatrist."

She spun on her heel and walked out.

The top leaflet was a friendly pale blue with a picture of a smiling kid. "*Hemophilia and Your Child,*" it said, in a large, comforting, sans-serif font. It assured Robert that advances in medical science meant that most hemophiliacs lived beyond adolescence. They led productive adult lives. No longer must a survivor be a landed noble; now, thanks to a shift away from farming and manufacturing, any hemophiliac could join normal society as an office worker, hopefully with medical benefits. Did Robert realize that he was protected by the Americans with Disabilities Act? He could demand safe alternatives to gym and playground equipment!

Robert tossed the leaflets onto the floor and went back to

Nothing in the Basement

switching channels with his safe, soft-buttoned remote control.

Chapter 41

When Sandra and Robert got home, Sandra went inside first and shooed the dogs onto the glass patio. Only after they were safely enclosed did she wave out the front door to Robert, who walked up the path as if the whole neighborhood was watching. It was, after all, Sunday. What else did the neighborhood have to do? They probably knew everything about the hospital stay. Someone knew someone who knew someone. They thought he was careless. Maybe infectious. He tried to walk nonchalantly, like a man coming home from the store. He wished he'd thought to have Sandra stop at a gas station, so that he could walk to the door with a full bag – something to throw people off. He had never met a neighborhood busybody, or even a neighbor, but he was sure they existed. Who else bought all the binoculars? Birdwatchers?

Safely inside, he sat at the kitchen table and drank a glass of orange juice. The dogs were hyper. He could see them through the glass. If they were human beings, they'd play tackle football and watch movie musicals. Robert liked them for that. They represented the stupidity that made America great – the kind of stupidity that invented rock and roll. The dogs did not give him the same regard. Perhaps they sensed that he was no longer a football man.

"Sorry," said Sandra. "I should really – they've been inside since yesterday."

Nothing in the Basement

"Oh, of course," said Robert. She slipped through the door, blocking the opening with her body, and closing it immediately after she cleared the threshold. The dogs jumped all over her. She swatted them down. She looked angry, but Robert knew from her eyebrows that it was an act. She let the dogs out the back door, and they immediately turned around to jump on her again. Robert watched the three roughhouse, and it seemed to him that Sandra had never really learned how to be rough. Maybe she didn't trust the sturdiness of the dogs. She was wrong. The dogs could take it.

He could feel creeping irritation. He wanted another glass of orange juice, but knew he would regret the acid. Instead, he pulled a magazine from the stack by the door. He only remembered subscribing to one, but they'd multiplied into a storm of automatic free offers and cross promotions. He got magazines for weight lifters, gun nuts, cigar lovers, weekend fishermen, even *House Beautiful* and *Ladies' Home Journal*. Perhaps Sandra had fallen victim to the same glossy conspiracy. Schoolchildren went door to door selling subscriptions. Sandra was a sucker for that trick. He sat down and flipped past the requisite seventy pages of cologne ads, careful to turn each page by sliding a finger along the center of the paper. He realized he was avoiding the edges for fear of paper cuts. He deliberately sliced his thumb with a Dolce & Gabbana full-page ad. It took several tries; the magazine had lost some of its sharpness to humidity. The cut hurt less than the ones he hadn't expected. It went straight down instead of shearing.

"Oh no!" said Sandra, sliding the patio door along its casters. "Let me get you a Band Aid."

Nothing in the Basement

"It's fine," said Robert. "I'm not going to bleed to death from a paper cut. And it's not like a Band Aid is going to stanch the wound. It's not magic. It's not vat-grown skin." She looked skeptical. He sighed. "Please get me a Band Aid," he said. By the time Sandra had returned, the cut had stopped bleeding.

"Do paper cuts usually bleed?" said Sandra. "It's stupid, but I don't remember. I feel like I always think 'oh, that's lucky, it hasn't broken skin,' but then there's a little red line the next day. You were bleeding."

"I'm not now," said Robert.

"Maybe we should leave the Band Aid off, so that if it starts bleeding again, we'll know. The Band Aid was a bad idea," said Sandra.

"Band Aids are great," said Robert. "They stop infection."

"I gave you the fabric kind since the cut is on your finger," said Sandra. "I know the fabric kind can get soggy, but the plastic one slides off, or they trap water and your finger goes wrinkly, and there are so many nerves there."

"I like the fabric kind," said Robert, who had no real preference.

"Should I make some tea?" said Sandra.

"About this hemophilia," said Robert. "I think I should get a second opinion."

"I couldn't agree more," said Sandra. "I checked the website of the CDC, and they say we should go to the hospital at the university. They have a whole ward."

"Okay," said Robert. "I guess I'll do that, then." They sat quietly for a few minutes.

"Did you know the CDC is based in Atlanta?" said Sandra. "It's so weird. You'd think if they were based anywhere, it would be here in DC. I think I thought the DC in CDC even stood for DC, even though I know it's Center for Disease Control. There being a center at all strikes me as strange, really, since it seems like you wouldn't want everyone to be in one place. You'd want them to be spread out. Basic epidemiology, don't you think?"

"Maybe you're mixing up the CDC and the National Institutes of Health," said Robert.

"That's probably it," said Sandra.

Chapter 42

Blood was a strange thing. After several days of thought, Sandra had failed to come up with a good metaphor. It didn't help that most metaphors which entered her head applied to kinship, and used blood as a metaphor for something else.

She tried to imagine explaining the circulatory system to a child. She vaguely remembered filmstrip animations from her own childhood which had relied heavily on freight trains and bus depots. It made a certain kind of sense. Busy roads, after all, were called arteries. Freeways were full of different vehicles, just like there were different kinds of blood cells. Cars left their houses (cells) and came back with groceries (nutrients). Sometimes, a road was blocked by construction, or by an accident, and the blood stopped. The city had a heart attack. Some blood might have four-wheel drive and ignore the speed limit.

That didn't really fit. Robert's blood didn't travel too fast. And if one car veered offroad and ran into a house, it wasn't followed by another car and another car until a police officer showed up to stop things. Maybe Robert's blood was more like airplanes. The mandated flight paths were invisible. Maybe Robert's blood cells were determined and loyal stunt fliers, like the Blue Angels. When one crashed and burned, the others followed, plunging their noses at high speeds into the ground.

Nothing in the Basement

Maybe Robert's veins were streams, but streams with only fish and no water. The fish slithered all over each other, slippery and sexual, until they suffocated.

That made no sense.

Sandra got out of bed and padded downstairs in the darkness. She sat, staring stupidly at the china cabinet, trying to remember where all the china had come from. Had she bought it herself? Had it been a grandmother's? At one point, she'd thought that she would use it every day. Mostly, it came out at Thanksgiving. Everyday use had gone out the window with Robert. Not because she thought he would break things, but because she'd be furious if he did.

She fished out a container of silver polish. She'd heard that toothpaste worked just as well, but she wasn't able to believe it. Silver polish was made for one task, toothpaste for another. It was one thing to use flour instead of cornmeal for gravy; it was another to replace beef with chicken in boeuf bourguignon – or to mold tofu to look like turkey. The right tool for the right task, thought Sandra. When she watched period pieces, her strongest emotional responses often occurred when a character removed a hat from a hat box of just the right size, or set a chalice in a perfectly carved niche.

Knives were first. Knives were easiest. Wrap a cloth, pinch, and slide. Sandra skipped forks on all but the most insomniac nights. Spoons were a pleasure and a torment. The edges of the bowl never seemed to go right, but she could rub gentle circles inside a spoon's smooth depression; she could work it like a worry stone.

Robert and Sandra fit together. She'd figured it out the first time she'd hugged him. He was the right height. His collarbone was the right curve. It meant something. When she stretched her arm along his arm, the dips matched.

Nothing in the Basement

Sandra wasn't one to believe in signs from heaven, but perfect fits were perfect fits, mystical or not. Never mind that people changed sizes. Never mind that she'd changed.

She looked at her face in the curve of the spoon. She knew that the small, inverted face peering up at her had thinner cheeks than her real face, a longer chin, deep-set eyes. It was her face as a skull. Her mind filled it out to a real Sandra, small and upside down. Upside-down Sandra wore a thunderous frown. Sandra smiled. The upside-down Sandra did not. Sandra brought her mouth into an even, straight-across line. The upside-down Sandra did not.

Sandra brought the spoon closer to her face. She rubbed it. She looked again. The upside-down Sandra looked over Sandra's shoulder. Sandra looked behind her. There was nothing there. The Sandra in the spoon seemed to raise her eyebrows. She very deliberately blinked. Sandra hadn't blinked. Sandra in the spoon mouthed something very clearly. Sandra reached up to check that her lips weren't moving. With her mouth covered, upside-down Sandra looked normal. Steady. Sandra's hand descended, and upside-down Sandra started mouthing again. Two syllables. That was all Sandra could make out. The first was a grimace – a long e? The second was a circle – a or o. Sandra tipped the spoon up and down – slid the face around for a better look. The first syllable was a sneer? The second was a Munch-inspired scream? The spoon started to ring.

"Nnnnn?" said Robert. He stood on the stairs, a blank expression on his face. It didn't look like a face at rest; it looked like a face of vulcanized rubber, able to flex under pressure, but bound to return to a pre-molded form. He looked at her and blinked. Sandra put the spoon back in its tray. She followed him back up to bed. When she woke up, she was sure the whole thing had been a dream. Robert didn't remember waking up. While he was in the shower, she fished out the spoon and ran her tongue along it, seeking a clue in the residue. She wondered what sleepwalking felt like.

The emptiness beneath the house had no thoughts or motivations. When you dug a hole, you made it. It helped no one and belonged to no one.

Chapter 43

The university hospital's waiting room hosted an odd mix. Some were clearly college students looking for doctors' notes to get out of class. It was an old scam, and a risky one. As an undergraduate at the same university, Robert had come in with the usual vague "dizzy, don't feel well" that worked with school nurses; he'd been put through a battery of allergy tests and an MRI. The hospital doctors – all researchers – were, after all, trained to discover Great Things in Unexpected Places. They had grants. They had his tuition money. When the doctors found nothing, they'd forced him to see a psychologist for two months. It was a very good hospital.

Aside from the students, the room was evenly split between the very affluent and the slightly down at heel. The former were there to pay for experimental treatments not yet approved by insurance companies. The latter were test cases in the paid studies the hospital was always running. Robert killed time by trying to guess their group assignments. The 30-year-old reading *The Unbearable Lightness of Being* was probably smoking cessation. The cheery older woman with the needlepoint – depression? Control group? She didn't seem sad – just gentle. Robert's experience of clinical depressives – straight depressives, not manic depressives, or depressives with OCD, or depressive alcoholics - was that they were extremely considerate. They spent more time sleeping than most people - qualities that Robert looked for in his friends. As a result, Robert felt that as unfortunate as depression was for the depressives, it was a pretty good deal for everyone else. He'd gotten good at spotting depressives and recruiting them to his work team, although he still hadn't figured out how to gracefully say, "I notice that you're probably a clinical depressive! I'm not, but we should hang out!" At times, he felt guilty about exploiting the mentally ill.

"Robert Brown?" A woman who was either a nurse, an orderly, or a pharmacist waved him through a door. Another woman drew blood from his arm and taped a cotton ball to the hole.

"You know, I just had a lot of blood pumped into me," said Robert. "I think it might throw things off."

"It shouldn't make a difference," said the woman. She made a note. Robert sat and waited for the doctor – damn cold as always. Robert suspected that sometime in the 1950s, a hospital administrator had walked into a grocery store and thought, "hmmmmm." Thenceforth, all hospital rooms and halls had been refrigerated to stop patients from spoiling.

The woman came back around the corner. "Why are you still here?" she said.

"I'm waiting for the doctor," said Robert.

"But the tests won't be ready for at least three hours," said the woman.

"Should I come back?" said Robert, but she had already disappeared. Robert found his way back to the waiting room, and out to the street. He walked to a burger place around the corner, and tried to make an order of French fries last as long as possible. He spent an hour working on a free Sudoku puzzle that was too hard for him – a stroke of luck – but ran out of distraction when he realized, with a fifth of the blanks filled in, that he'd made a logic error he couldn't locate. Stupid.

He walked back to the waiting room. Nothing was ready. The magazines were either old or about golfing. He left again; wandered around campus, hoping he'd run into a protester on a soapbox, or an aspiring folk singer, or even a religious group handing out free little green bibles. Nothing. He read the flyers for upcoming events. He read the notice about how to report a sexual assault. He read the student newspaper and tried to savor "your voice" responses to the mascot's new costume. Robert's vote, costume unseen: give him a horse as a sidekick, and let him use his real hands instead of those spongy gloves.

He returned to the waiting room.

The doctor was at lunch. The rest of the day was very busy. Could he come in tomorrow?

"I could die," lied Robert. The receptionist looked unconvinced, but said that all right, if he wanted to wait, she'd fit him in if someone canceled. The doctor was a specialist, she said, as though he should understand. It meant that he was supposed to go away quietly. To hell with that, thought Robert. He navigated through several unique hallways (either the building had seen extensive and staggered renovation, or each department had its own decorating budget) until he homed in on the gift shop. He managed to buy a paperback about conspiracies, stolen submarines, and a sexy Russian double agent. It was not *The Hunt for Red October*, but the cover design clearly hoped he would mistake it for Tom Clancy. It was also not sold for the cover price; the hospital benefited from a hefty markup. On another day, Robert would have put the book back and left. Today, it seemed fitting. Inevitable.

Nothing in the Basement

As soon as he returned to the waiting room, the receptionist lit into him.

"Where have you been?" she said. "The doctor has been waiting. I *hope* there's still time."

"I thought the doctor was at lunch," said Robert.

"In here," said the receptionist.

The doctor was younger than Robert. He was very tan. He shook Robert's hand with a big smile.

"How can I help you out today?" he said.

"Well," said Robert, "I wanted a second opinion about my hemophilia. My supposed hemophilia."

"What do you mean?" said the doctor. His brow was attractively creased. His eyes held just the right twinkling concern.

"I'm going to cut to the chase," said Robert.

"Please," said the doctor. "Feel free."

"I don't think I'm a hemophiliac. That is, I wasn't before last week."

"Well," said the doctor, "it seems like you have two different points of discussion, if I understand you correctly. When you say that you weren't a hemophiliac before last week, you may mean, without realizing it, that before last week, you never suffered from the effects of hemophilia – your body compensated in some way, and is no longer compensating. Since you never suffered symptoms, you were never tested, and never diagnosed. In that sense, you are right. The disease model of diagnosis doesn't properly fit the circumstances. For example, at any time, I could place my foot incorrectly and break my ankle. My ankle is not now broken, but it has a latent possibility of breaking. If I wanted to, I could refer to it as a non-manifesting broken ankle, or a broken ankle in remission. Doctors sometimes pathologize patients unnecessarily. It's a failing that we should be more aware of. Thank you."

Robert opened his mouth, but the doctor continued.

"On the other hand, you may mean that if we had tested you for hemophilia two weeks ago, we would not have found hemophilia. The suggestion is unlikely, but if it were true, it would open up new avenues of research. Perhaps new cures. If you were able to present evidence of spontaneous hemophilia – or if, in contrast, you were to cease being hemophiliac now that you have been tested – that would be tremendously interesting, and I hope that I would have the opportunity to explore it with the help of grants.

"However, in the meantime, without evidence, I would like to address your first concern, which is the question of whether you are a hemophiliac. If you like, I can take you through the blood work, but I think you'll find the information fairly simple. Hemophilia simply means that your body does not manufacture enough of a certain clotting factor – in your case, factor eight. We know that the factor is low because we have looked at your blood and it is not there, not in the amount we expect to see. Even if you have lost blood recently, it should not change the proportion of factor eight. I know that you were given blood, and quite a lot of it, but if anything, that should make your factor eight readings *higher*, because the blood you were given did not come from a hemophiliac. Do you understand what I'm telling you?"

"I have hemophilia," said Robert.

"Yes," said the doctor. "I'm sorry."

"What should I do?" said Robert.

"For now, unfortunately," said the doctor, "you're in a difficult situation. There are prophylactic measures we can take – you can come in for an injection of factor eight on a regular basis, which will also let us keep track of you. It will be more of a hassle than a dental checkup, but it will mean you can live a fairly normal life. It's very much like being a diabetic who needs insulin. If you explain it to people in that way, they'll be less frightened. I'm sorry that I can't tell you how much the injections will cost; I won't know until we've started treating you. You may not need injections very often; you may need them almost every day. It depends on your body and how it responds. I think it is very likely that we can cover or at least defray the cost of your injections, due to how old you are. The fact is, we don't have many people your age who we can study. We have only had reliable factor eight for a few decades, and we unfortunately lost a lot of patients to AIDS. You have potential as a resource, crass as it sounds.

"However, and this is why I say 'unfortunately,' none of that can start for a few months. Lots of paperwork. Until then, I'm afraid you'll have to rely on emergency room visits. Given that you went so long without needing one, I don't think you're looking at too great a risk. With another patient, I might suggest paying out of pocket to cover the gap, but I think you'll be fine. Of course, if there's another episode like the last one, please come back in and I'll see what I can do."

The doctor smiled and waited with an open and concerned expression.

"So I can ... be normal?" said Robert. "But not for another few months?"

"You can 'be normal' now, for the most part," said the doctor. "No contact sports. No martial arts. Be sensible in your sexual practices, by which I mean no blood play and no spanking. If you nick yourself while shaving, you'll be fine. It's not that your blood doesn't clot at all, you understand. It simply clots very slowly. Apply pressure to small wounds, elevate them above the heart. The usual. Watch out for internal bleeding. If you notice swelling in your joints, or blood in your eye, or unusual bruising, please go to the hospital immediately. Immediately."

"I will," said Robert. "Thank you."

"Please be sure your address is correct with the receptionist," said the doctor. "I look forward to seeing you soon." He shook Robert's hand again in a practiced and reassuring manner.

"He's really very good," Robert said to the receptionist. "I imagine it cuts down on the malpractice lawsuits."

"There are no malpractice lawsuits," said the receptionist.

"That's what... Never mind," said Robert.

Chapter 44

On the way to rehearsal, Robert struggled with what to tell the cast. He didn't want to seem weird. At the same time, he didn't want to lose his life to a stage slap because he was too macho to let on that he was sick. Maybe he could pretend to have another disease. Maybe he could pretend to have Lou Gehrig's disease. It was appropriately deadly and mysterious. Alas, he did not have the background knowledge required to pull it off – he knew the real name was ALS, but not what it stood for. One slightly better-informed cast mate, and the jig would be up.

He found the director at the Coke machine. "Hey," he said, "this is awkward, but I've got a health problem that's flaring up, and my doctor has asked me to avoid anything that could cause bruising, at least until he gives me the go ahead. I, uh, can't do the fight scene or the bit where I get tied up."

"Do you have a note from this so-called doctor?" the director said. "What kind of health problem dares stand in the way of a sword fight?"

"Hemophilia," said Robert.

"Ooooooh - blood effects," said the director. "Fair enough – don't tell me. And let me think about what we can do. Maybe you're a comic, limp-wristed villain? Maybe you have a henchman? Magical powers?" He shook the Coke can absentmindedly. He walked into the rehearsal room and clapped his hands.

"People," he said, "we've got work to do. It's not your fault – it's mine. The villain stuff has gotten stale. I think we all like Robert too much. We're getting complacent. I'm going to change it up, see what I like. Places for scene two."

After rehearsal, the director accepted praise for his bravery and creativity.

"As fun as stage combat is," said the heroine, "I never really believe it, you know? I've seen far too many slaps that don't quite connect. And it always drains the tension out. This is sooooo creepy. Action over a distance. Have you been watching Fritz Lang?"

"It was all Robert's idea," said the director. "Entirely. Especially the chicken."

"You liar," said Robert.

Chapter 45

Midway through the afternoon, Sandra's boss called her into the office.

"You missed more work last week," he said.

"I know," said Sandra. "I'm so sorry. I called in, but I'm sorry. I know that doesn't make up for it. I had to take Robert to the hospital. I can get a doctor's note. I was worried. You can dock me a day's pay. You should. I'll do free overtime next week."

"That's not necessary," said Sandra's boss. "Can I offer you some water?"

"No thank you," said Sandra, throat suddenly dry. "I mean, yes, please, yes." He poured a glass from the pitcher on his desk and slid it over.

"Relax," said her boss. "You're not fired. I called you in to see how you're doing. It seems like you've had a rough time lately. I'm worried about you. You doing okay, buddy?"

Sandra's eyes got wet. It was horrifying. "Oh, you know," she said. "I'm okay."

"You are," said her boss. "You're doing just fine." He passed her a box of Kleenex. "I'm not trying to pressure you into disclosing anything personal. This company respects your privacy. We are glad to have you here, working. But I want you to know that our office has a bereavement policy, and you may qualify for paid family leave. Would you like me to tell you more about the program?" He sounded like he was reading from a script learned at a management retreat. The expression on his face was nervous but proud, as though he'd spent decades as a volunteer fire marshal and had now, unexpectedly, been able to use Star Wars trivia to save a group of kidnapped schoolchildren.

"I think," said Sandra, "I think thank you, but I'm really – I really just want to work."

"Great," said her boss. "If you change your mind, or if your situation changes, the policy is clearly described in the quote 'boring' section of the employee handbook. We understand that things happen outside of our employees' control. All we ask is that you keep us in the loop."

Sandra nodded and started to stand.

"Sandra," said her boss. "I'm serious. Think about this, okay? I know you're worried to say anything that might endanger a promotion, but I can tell you privately that you could request two years off, and you'd get it. At your level, it's still cheaper than recruiting and training a permanent replacement. That's unofficial, and if you tell anyone I promised you anything, I will deny it categorically."

Sandra nodded. When she got back to her desk, she couldn't get the computer monitor to stop swimming around, so she went to the bathroom and shut herself in a stall. "One, two, three," she silently counted, swabbing her eyes with toilet paper. "One, two, three."

On the way home, Sandra stopped by an antique store and fondled the small drawers of two-hundred-year-old lingerie chests, imagining a life full of hand-stitched silk panties, embroidered garters, and scented letters from secret admirers. The store owners let her browse for fifteen minutes past closing time, but kicked her out when they saw she wasn't going to buy anything. She went to the restaurant next door, ordered stuffed jalapeño peppers to go, and ate them in her car. At home, she skipped dinner because she didn't feel well. Robert ate soup.

Chapter 46

Thump! Pilgrim ran at the door. Thump! Robert growled and shook a pink rubber toy back and forth. Thump! Robert set the toy on the floor. Pilgrim sat down and wagged his tail. Robert picked up the toy. Thump!

In the rules of the game, as far as Robert could tell. Pilgrim would pretend the glass door was not there, and a toy on the floor was successfully his. He was also allowed to pretend that Robert did not exist, and the toy floated on its own. Empty hand? Nothing doing. Pilgrim would lose interest and wander off. It had taken Robert several days to figure out the game. When they were not playing it, he hid the toy behind his section of the bookshelf so that Sandra would not return it to the dogs' toy basket, in the patio room where Robert could not now go without a deadly risk of a dog jumping on him. In each round of the game, Robert would lift the toy until it was near his face and say, "Up here, boy! Look over here!" Pilgrim never met his eyes. He just barked happily at the toy.

"I see how it is," said Robert. "Now that I don't feed you anymore, I'm not interesting?"

It made him angry, but he kept playing.

Most of his life felt that way. He hadn't had sex since his diagnosis. Actually, he had, twice, but there had been something pathetic about it, like hospice care. He'd started going to bed a little early or a little late so that he or Sandra was already sleepy by the time the other got there. He'd sneak upstairs to brush his teeth long before he was ready to retire, so that he could better control the timing. As he brushed, he tried to ignore his irritation at the new soft-bristled toothbrush.

"Stop barking at Robert," said Sandra. She had walked into the kitchen.

"It's okay," said Robert. "It's a game."

"Barking?" said Sandra. "Okay."

She slid open the door and shimmied through.

"Come on!" she said, voice still bright through the glass. The dogs gleefully followed her into the yard. Watching through the door and the patio glass, Robert felt as though he was trapped behind an aquarium. Not in an aquarium, but behind one. On the other side of an airlock.

He was losing her. She didn't know it; he didn't think she had plans. But he was losing her. Maybe his illness would speed it up, or it would slow it down. He wasn't sure. Probably slow it down. Sandra was a worrier. She sent money during telethons about kids in Africa or Muscular Dystrophy. Pity would make her stay, if he managed to seem grateful instead of angry. Even if he failed at gratitude, she wouldn't leave for at least a year, he thought – she'd be too concerned over how it would look.

To win her back, he'd have to display strength and heroism. She might say she wanted something else, but she didn't. She wanted to be... She was a peculiarly difficult woman to woo. She wanted someone who would take all her worries away, but who didn't make her feel un-feminist or unnecessary. She wanted grand romantic gestures, but not surprises. Robert suspected that everything would be much easier if he had lots of money. Lots of money. And prestige.

Nothing in the Basement

He should get some. In the meantime, he needed to act strong and heroic and pathetic and ailing enough for Sandra to stay long enough for his heroic stoicism to seduce her. God damn it. Should he let her in on his deep feelings? Should he avoid disclosure, as it would arouse her compassion but damp her libido?

In the yard, Sandra fought Trixie for a stick. Sandra would let Trixie think she had it, and then she'd pull again and drag her a few feet.

I deserve better than this, Robert thought. I'm a good man. Maybe I'm not perfect, but I deserve dignity. I work hard. I read the paper. I vote in even the minor elections. I don't drink too much. I don't gamble. I do the dishes. I take care of my skin. At a funeral, I find the right thing to say. I tell jokes at parties, and they're not off color. The women laugh as much as the men. My work is, in a very real sense, saving the environment – saving the entire planet. The databases are going to save the world. And I never brag about it. I never bring my stress home. I don't drink too much, and when I do drink, it makes me silly – never mean. I hold myself to the highest standard. I couldn't live my life compromised. The highest standard. What makes it so hard to love me? What kind of person is so incapable of love?

I should leave her, he thought. That shit with Virginia. Or the year before, when she threw a fit at my sister's anniversary party because she thought my cousin was hitting on her. Which he was – he's a creep – but Jesus. She could have just avoided the cousin instead of freezing up and attacking everyone and offending my sister and mother and god knew who else. When had she ever defended *him*? At what coworker party hadn't she left him standing in a corner? At what point had she stuck up for him when her

143

sorority sisters settled in for a round of man bashing?

I should get out while the getting is good, he thought. Leave her the house and the mortgage and just get out. Move to an apartment in the city and get back to eating genuinely spicy food, and not the bland shit that Sandra called spicy. Listen to fucking rock music. Stop getting needled over whether he'd put both athletic socks into the same wash load, or whether he'd properly wrapped the onion before putting it in the fridge. Maybe spend too much on lunch without grief. Fuck it. He was leaving, and if anybody had shit to say about it, well – he had hemophilia.

In the yard, Sandra stepped backward, and abruptly vanished into a hole in the ground. Trixie let go of the stick.

Chapter 47

Sandra had never liked roller coasters. This was no surprise to anyone; it didn't even bear announcing. However, the reason was not a dislike of adrenaline, or a weak stomach, or an overactive imagination. She'd witnessed a county fair midway accident in which three people died. Even that hadn't made an impression.

What Sandra hated about roller coasters:

1. Waiting in line
2. In the sun
3. In order to be snapped into restraints that didn't fit.

She also hated the sound of metal on metal. She had never liked trains, although she used them. Used wooden spoons to stir metal pots; used plastic lids on metal cans; used porcelain plates with metal forks. Used dull knives instead of knife sharpeners. With the clanking of metal chains and the susurrus of metal rails, how could anyone enjoy a roller coaster? How could anyone fly free of gravity with the reminder of weight, of cages, of metal? Slicing? Being pushed through a grille?

When Sandra fell through the lawn, her first thought was, "you see? Why not like *this*?" She dropped ten feet, and it was like being bounced on a parachute. Once she and the ground came to rest, she walked toward the edge of the newly-created hole. The turf beneath her feet undulated like a waterbed. Which, she realized, turf should not do. Turf could not undulate unless there was nothing underneath it. How much nothing? Decades ago, thirty miles north, a section of highway had collapsed under a car. Cavers had to bring up the driver's body. Sinkholes riddled Maryland. Some ran to ten feet. Some to a hundred.

Sandra dug her fingers into the stretched grass at the side of the hole and felt stone. Limestone, she thought, or something similar. She thought she could scramble up the side with a gentler incline. She would get one chance, probably, and if her grip failed or the turf gave way, she would slide back fast enough to break through the crust at the bottom. She would fall. Who knew how far.

Trixie's head poked over the edge. She whined. She backed away. With a sinking feeling, Sandra realized that Trixie was preparing to jump down and rescue her.

"Trixie," she called out in her sweetest voice. Trixie's head reappeared. It looked long-suffering. Sandra grabbed the stick, which had fallen with her, and flung it as hard as she could. Trixie disappeared in a flurry of offended barks.

Sandra gripped the side of the wall and pulled. She turned her thankfully bare feet sideways, and shuffled into second position. She felt like a character in an old arcade game. She tried to embrace two-dimensionality.

"Surface area," thought Sandra. "I love surface area. I love coefficients of friction. I am a mosquito on the surface of the water. I have the Zen mind of a sticky potholder."

Inch by inch, she shimmied up the wall. It reminded her of climbing door frames – chimneying, she thought climbers called it, but not chimneying – chimneying doorframes was easy. You just turned your body into an expandable pole, like chin-up bars you could buy in *Men's Health*, or the spit that held the toilet paper roll. This was not a chimney. She was a spider. She wondered whether when she stopped climbing, her arms would float into the air.

"Sandra?" called Robert, from far away. "I'm in the house. I'm at the upstairs window. I think I can throw you something. Is there something I can throw you? Are you alive? How far down are you? Is anything broken? I'm calling 911."

"Don't throw anything," said Sandra. She pulled herself over the edge. In a flash of inspiration, she decided to keep crawling until she reached the house. "Like a gentle soldier," she thought. "Like a discreet policeman."

"Who should I call?" said Robert, still at the upstairs window. Sandra stood. She rustled the dogs back into the patio. She dangled treats until they came. She looked back at her lawn, half of which was now somewhere between a crater and a ravine.

Sandra got angry. "Wait right there," said Sandra. "I will be back in a minute." She rushed through the house like a storm cloud, and overturned tool benches in the garage until she found a long-handled shovel. She reemerged.

"I am tired of being pushed around," she yelled at the sinkhole. "I am going to kill you."

"Sandra," said Robert, "I don't think..."

"You stay there," she said. "I am doing this. Call 911 if something happens." She edged out onto the lawn, prodding the ground before her with the shovel. She felt blind. She felt like she was picking up trash in the park. She felt like she wanted a metal detector and a divining rod.

She made it to the edge of the depression. She hefted the shovel and began cutting. Halfway around, the turf plug broke loose. It slid a few feet deeper into the hole. Between the grass at the top of the hole and the grass at the bottom, the sides were sandy.

"I'm going down," said Sandra. "Call my name every five minutes. If twice in a row I don't answer, call 911."

"This is suicidal," said Robert. "Please."

Sandra slid into the hole. Now that the grass had come loose, she could see that it was an irregular shape. There were corners – indentations. Vertices. She wedged herself into one, bracing with her feet. She extended the shovel and jabbed. The edge of the shovel went through. The grass slid down another foot.

"Sandra," called Robert.

"Yep," called Sandra. She made a mental note to buy walkie-talkies. You thought you didn't need them if you had cell phones. It wasn't the same.

Sandra's cell phone rang. Robert's ring.

"I'm not answering," called Sandra. The phone stopped ringing.

"I just wanted to see if it would work," called Robert.

Sandra descended. Wedged herself in again. Poked. Soil came loose under her foot and she slid a little before she could stop herself.

"Sandra?" said Robert. He was hard to hear. You forgot that sound was a wave. It traveled, like light, in a straight line. Twenty more feet, and she'd be out of Robert's cone. Ridiculous. She sang the chorus of "Deck the Halls." She let the fa-la-las echo.

"I'm going to be another hour," she called. "Forget about the five minute thing. I'll be back in an hour."

Silence.

"Okay?" said Sandra.

Nothing in the Basement

Silence.

"Robert?"

"I'm calling," said Robert.

"Just watch TV for an hour," said Sandra. "It will be nothing."

Silence.

"I refuse to be scared of my backyard," said Sandra. Her legs were starting to hurt. "I am going to get to the bottom of this. So help me."

No response. This far down, the hole was narrow. Not all of it, but Sandra's preferred defilade. She shifted so her back was against one wall and her legs stretched in front of her. Much better, she thought. It's like swimming - or floating. You switch strokes every once in a while so that muscles can rest. Easy as pie. The new position allowed her to descend rather quickly. The turf plug had fallen away. She wished she'd brought a flashlight. She debated for a minute, then dropped the shovel. One Mississippi. Two Mississippi. How many seconds times nine-point-eight meters per second per second? What was the mass of the shovel? Did she need to know the mass of the shovel?

Sandra's special chute had ended. She was well clear of topsoil. The walls were layered rock. "I bet I could find fossils," Sandra thought. Then: "They look like stacked-up pancakes. A kid has stuck his finger into stony pancakes, and I am a pat of butter melting my way down." Her sweat felt greasy. She looked up at the sky. There wasn't much of it. "I should head back up," she thought. She slid a foot onto a thin ledge, and slid around to another chimney. She wasn't sure that the ledge would support her weight. Her heart was pounding. She made it. She braced herself and closed her eyes.

Nothing in the Basement

"All the way to China," she thought. "Isn't that the joke? A hole all the way to China." She wanted to go back up. She did not want to reattempt the ledge. She descended.

Where did it all go – the previous soil? No part of the lawn had risen. No mountain had grown down the street. The land had somehow seeped away, like an hourglass. How long had it taken for groundwater to erode it? What kind of runoff had etched its way through? You could use all the organic fertilizer you wanted. It didn't make a damn difference. You could compost. The soil didn't care. Not this far down. The rock didn't care.

Sandra could feel the hole widen. It smelled salty. Mineral. It smelled like Mars.Something slithered past her. It was too dark to see. Then it got very bright – too bright. "I'm being Raptured," Sandra thought. "I have been bitten by a deep-earth coral snake."

"Ma'am," called a deep male voice, "are you able to move?"

"Within limits," said Sandra. Her eyes adjusted to the flashlight beam.

"Grab the rope and wrap it around your hips," said the voice. "Make yourself a little seat, like a rope swing. Can you do that? Have you made a rope swing before?"

"A long time ago," said Sandra.

"The thing to do is go crazy with the knots," said the voice. "We don't ever want those suckers to come undone. We want to have to cut them off you. Do you know how to tie knots?"

"Sort of," said Sandra.

"Have you done any sailing? Camping? Were you in Girl Scouts?"

"I used to sew."

"Okay," said the voice. "Okay. Tie those knots real tight. Give yourself some fail safes. We're not going to pull until you say you're ready, and I don't want you to say you're ready until you're secure, okay?"

"Okay," said Sandra. "I'm ready."

"Are you sure?" said the voice.

"I'm sure," said Sandra.

"Okay," said the voice. "We're going to start pulling really easy. I want you to put your feet on the wall and walk your way up. You can hold on to the rope with your hands. Can you do that?"

"Okay," said Sandra.

"We're going to pull now," said the voice.

Ten minutes later, Sandra was blinking in sunlight while an EMT prodded her and a burly man from the fire department gave her contact information for the Environmental Protection Agency's Maryland Bureau and the county geologic survey. Before they left, they made her promise to wrap up in blankets and drink hot tea with lots of sugar.

Robert was ashy faced. He was crying.

"What if I lost you?" he said. "What if you'd died and I'd never see you again?"

Chapter 48

When the curtain went down at the end of the play, Robert didn't remember any of the previous two hours. He remembered putting on stage makeup. He remembered asking a cast mate whether he had enough eyeliner. After that, a blank. The curtain came up again, and with the rest of the cast, he walked out to effusive applause. Someone presented the director with a bouquet of roses.

"Did I remember all of my lines?" Robert asked the stage manager. She groaned with the pleased and annoyed expression intellectuals wear upon hearing an egregious pun.

"See you at the cast party?" she said.

"Of course!" said Robert. "See you there." He shook his head. He changed out of costume. Sandra was waiting in the auditorium.

"That seemed fun," said Sandra. "I'm not really a good judge of these things, but it seemed like a good production. I liked the ribbon stuff in the lady's costume. People laughed a lot at your lines. Could you hear them on stage?"

"I didn't hear anything," Robert said.

"Well, they were laughing," said Sandra. Her eyebrows drew together slightly. "It was supposed to be funny, right? And scary? Funny and also scary?"

"Yes," said Robert. "That is how it was supposed to be."

"Oh good," said Sandra.

Nothing in the Basement

Robert wasn't sure of the rules for cast parties, so he dawdled at the liquor store. He was relieved to see cars parked up and down the street around the party house. It allowed Sandra's usual exit strategy - show up right as the party starts swinging, have one drink, tell everyone how great they are, and depart. Robert stayed late and took cabs home.

A cheer erupted when Robert and Sandra entered. Most came from the leading man.

"I nearly lost it when you said 'my indomitable philter' tonight. How many times have we rehearsed that scene, and you still crack me up! You are the master!"

"'I have it on the authority of certain fiendish pigmies...'" Robert quoted in a nasal voice. He could feel Sandra rolling her eyes. The leading lady wrapped her arms around Robert and kissed him on the cheek. She did the same to Sandra.

"It's so great that you're so cool," she effused to Sandra. "Sometimes wives can be a little, but you're not at all. It's awesome. Rock it!"

Later, Robert cornered the actress, mainly by agreeing to do shots of a vile blue liquid which no one but her would drink.

"Can I ask you something?" he said.

"Shoot," said the actress. She laughed. "Double entendre." She laughed. "But seriously."

"In our scene, did I seem all there? I mean, did I seem entirely present, or was there a certain absence in my face?"

"Oh, sweetie," she said, setting down her drink, "don't do this to yourself. You can't start second guessing. If you start worrying whether every moment is your best moment – whether you delivered a line better weeks ago in rehearsal – you'll go crazy. You were good. You were on. You nearly cracked Steve up. I could see it happen. That's real."

"I don't want you to think I'm fishing for compliments," said Robert.

"You don't have to fish," she said. She smiled.

"Hey," he said. "You know I'm still pretty new to acting."

"You could have fooled me," she said. "You're a natural."

"Have you ever lost yourself in a role?" he asked. "I mean completely forgotten who you were when you were performing?"

"You're talking about possession," she said. "Yeah. It happens sometimes. It's rare. I've only managed it a couple of times, but those were my best performances. I know it's not like that for everyone, but I don't know. I think it's really special. Don't assume it's going to happen every time."

"Neat," said Robert. "Thanks."

What a relief.

"One time," said the actress, "I was playing Medea – this was a summer stock production – and it was like I was watching the whole performance. I was, like, floating in my head, watching as I raised my hand. I just gave my body over to this other person – to Medea."

"You were there, though," said Robert.

"I was there. I was playing Medea. Have I had waaaaaaay too many shots?"

"Nah," said Robert. "I wouldn't do any more, though."

"Okay," said the actress. "I think I'm going to go to the bathroom now."

"Good idea," said Robert.

On the cab ride home, the sugar started to jangle in Robert's system. How many times had he blacked out, he wondered. Gone through a day without anyone noticing? He'd heard of it as a side effect to sleeping pills, so it had to be possible. Had he driven asleep? Eaten lunch asleep when he thought he'd skipped lunch? It was spooky. There had to be a way to test, short of wiring himself with closed circuit television cameras. Dictaphone? Pocket notebook. Everything seemed annoyingly tedious. He shouldn't worry about it. If no one had ever noticed, it had to be doing no harm. If Sandra had noticed, he'd have heard about it. Endlessly. He fell asleep in the cab, and the driver had to knock on the glass to wake him. Robert guessed that he'd driven the block a few extra times, but he didn't begrudge him.

Chapter 49

At the grocery store, Sandra avoided the cereal aisle. It wasn't the cereal so much as the boxes. She loved the puzzles. She loved the trivia. She had debated whether the Trix rabbit or the Lucky Charms leprechaun would win in a fight. When she had lived alone, she had held on to commemorative boxes – cereal endorsed by favorite Olympic gymnasts, one-time cereals released as movie tie-ins, and her personal favorite, a series of boxes made to look as thought they'd "fallen through time," which firmly established that Sugar-Os had existed in both Victorian London and ancient Egypt. Cereal, Sandra would take or leave. Dry, it broke into shards, stabbed you in the mouth. Wet, it turned to mush. For decades, Sandra had stuck to oatmeal, which was mushy to begin with. Sandra had thrown out all of her cereal boxes the month before her wedding (except for a few she sold to fellow collectors). Nevertheless, the cereal aisle was a risk, if only for the nostalgia.

Today, however, a neighbor was in the cereal aisle, and Sandra couldn't tell whether she'd been spotted. If she walked by the aisle without stopping, she might be unfriendly, engaged in deliberate avoidance. If, on the other hand, she made a show of recognition, she might look desperate. Sandra weighed her options. The woman's cart held only a few items, and the woman had a large cart. The woman had plans. Of the possible settings for light small talk, the cereal aisle seemed promising. It was not the refrigerated section. Their carts would not cause a major disruption. It was vastly superior to the checkout line, where conversation would have to continue until one of them reached the front of the line. In the cereal aisle, Sandra could gaze at the box designs.

She turned her cart and browsed the more serious granola products.

"Why, Sandra," said the neighbor, "I almost didn't notice you there. I love your hair."

"Thank you," said Sandra. "I like the sequins on your sweater."

"Isn't it fun?" said the neighbor. She grabbed a box of Frosted Mini Wheats. "Can I ask you – I don't mean to pry, but have you been having trouble with your yard?"

"What do you mean?" said Sandra, face carefully blank. The geologic survey team would not examine the crater until the following week, and they had asked her not to start a panic. The request had struck her as an absurd government cover up – possibly in collaboration with housing developers, mining companies, and insurance underwriters. Couldn't sinkholes be caused by sewage leaks?

Sandra looked at the woman in front of her, and she took the government's viewpoint. One word to this scion of suburban gate keeping, and Sandra could terrify the whole neighborhood. It was a heady power, the exercise of which would require Sandra to participate in gossip sessions. People she didn't like would ask her to organize protests; to appear as an angry martyr at protests.

"Have you been having trouble with *your* yard?" Sandra asked the woman. Sandra thought the question was a good balance of concern and aggression. For good measure, she added: "I heard there might be moles moving in."

"Gracious!" said the woman. "I had not heard that. Thank you. I haven't had any moles, but I must admit, my yard is miserable from all this heat – my azaleas are positively droopy."

"Oh, the ones in front look lovely," said Sandra.

"You mean the ones on the side," corrected the woman. "The front is all ferns this year."

"Yes," said Sandra. "That's what I meant."

"I just saw your husband out front yesterday working on that hackberry tree. In the morning, you know, I jog, before it gets hot. Before it gets light out, sometimes! But not in the summer – I don't want you thinking I rise that early! Your husband is very smart to do his yard labor then. He's an engineer or something, isn't he? He has the look. And on a workday! That's a hard worker you've got."

"Yes," said Sandra. "He's very dedicated." She had no idea what the woman could possibly be talking about.

"I mean, he was just attacking that hackberry. He looked like he was trying to strangle it. It must have him pretty frustrated!"

"Oh, it does," said Sandra. "It definitely does."

"I didn't want to intrude while he was working. Never sneak up on a man with an axe, my mama said. Not that I could see his axe, but you know. But I wanted to give you something." The woman fished in a large needlepoint purse and reemerged with a business card.

"Here," she said. "It's my son-in-law's business. He's a landscaper. You can't tell from my yard, because I insist on doing all my own work like a stubborn crazy person..."

Sandra cooed, as required, that no, the yard was beautiful, a joy to pass, and you liked to see a woman so active and involved in the maintenance of her property.

"... but he really does do good work. He can have that old hackberry out in a flash. They use backhoes, you know. Maybe you'd like to put in a chestnut, get your bulbs in nice and early so you can have tulips next spring. I do love a tulip, not that you'd know. Although I hear vegetable gardens are quite the thing – more in the back, though. Anyway, give him a call, if you want to. Don't tell him I've been nagging you!"

"You're very kind," said Sandra, although she wasn't sure how this was true. She turned into the snack food aisle, careful to look cheery until she had safely rounded the corner. She pulled out her cell phone.

"Hey, babe," said Robert.

"I know this is random, but did you choke the hackberry tree this morning? Or any morning?" said Sandra.

There was a pause. When Robert started talking again, his voice was earnest. "Please don't think I'm shooting you down," he said. "I think this is a tremendous gesture. But it's not a good time for me – I just ate. If you call back in literally half an hour, I am ready to go."

"What?" said Sandra.

"I'm really sorry," said Robert. "I love you."

"Do you need to get off the phone?" said Sandra.

"No, not at all," said Robert. "I just can't talk dirty right now."

"Okay," said Sandra. "Literally. Literally did you walk out into the front yard at some point and attack the very real and literal tree that is in the front yard?"

"Why would I do that?" said Robert.

"I don't know," said Sandra. "That was my next question."

Nothing in the Basement

"Well, I didn't," said Robert. "Are you out front? Is there something wrong with the tree?"

"I'm at the grocery store," said Sandra.

"Would you get some of those crackers I like?" said Robert. "I'm out."

"Why didn't you write it on the list?" said Sandra.

"Jesus," said Robert. "I just ran out. I told you I just ate. I just ate. And I ate crackers, and I'm out. Okay?"

"Fine. I'll get the crackers," said Sandra. "I love you."

"I love you, too," said Robert. He hung up the phone. He walked outside and casually picked up stray weeds and bits of plastic until he was fairly sure the block was unoccupied. He sauntered to the hackberry tree, oozing unconcern, and ran his hand up and down the bark. He felt no recognition. A few sections of trunk were oddly smooth, and others were chipped, but Robert knew nothing about trees. He did not, in fact, care about plants you could not eat, unless they smelled particularly nice. Hackberry bark might look smooth all of the time. He had no other hackberries to compare it to. There could be wild animals coming through every day, rubbing against the tree. His front yard could be the center of a migratory pilgrimage for deer. Unless the animals made it to the backyard, Robert would remain in the dark.

Robert carefully examined the honeysuckle, so that if someone was watching, his attention to the hackberry would not be construed as confirmation of whatever it was that had Sandra concerned. He was simply a man in his front yard, picking up trash and checking on the plants. He waved to a kid on a bike, who ignored him. He stuck his hands in his pockets and nodded.

Chapter 50

Robert sat at the kitchen table. In front of him, he had a digital watch with a timer built in (as well as an alarm, and water resistance to two hundred feet), a slender sewing needle with athletic tape wrapped around the eye, a cotton ball, a paper towel, a number-two pencil, a small blue notebook, and a plastic bottle full of rubbing alcohol. Robert soaked the cotton ball with alcohol, then rubbed the needle tip around on the cotton ball. He laid his left arm on the table, palm side up. He jabbed the needle three millimeters into his wrist, halfway between his tendons. With his right hand, he started the timer. He removed the needle.

For a moment, he saw no injury. Then, a small red dot appeared. Robert blotted it away. Another dot appeared. Robert blotted it away. Sandra came down the stairs.

"What are you doing?" she said.

"Shh," said Robert. He swabbed. A small red dot appeared.

"Did you cut yourself?" said Sandra.

"It's an experiment," said Robert. "I don't want to raise my heart rate."

"Let me get you a Band Aid," said Sandra.

"No," said Robert. "It's an experiment. Shhhh." Sandra stood silently in the doorway until Robert swabbed and a red dot did not appear. He stopped the timer. He wrote a number down in the notebook.

Nothing in the Basement

"How many numbers are in that book?" said Sandra.

"Thirteen," said Robert. "But two of them are junk data – I had wine with dinner on Thursday. One time last week I think I went in at an angle."

"This strikes me as not very safe," said Sandra.

"It's fine," said Robert. "It's a little improvised, but I'm proud of my setup. I do clean my arm beforehand, if that's worrying you."

"No," said Sandra. "I'm worried about nerve damage. I'm … what if you lose the use of your hands?"

"That's not going to happen," said Robert. "I know you want to live in a super safe world where everything is super safe, but this is safe. And it's good for science."

"How?" said Sandra. "How is it good for science? How is this not you acting crazy?"

"Sandra," said Robert, "I am curious about the world around me. And in me. It's healthy."

"You are going to get tetanus, or collapse a vein, or scar your arm up until you look like a junkie," said Sandra. "This has to stop."

"I'm flattered by your concern," said Robert. "But, really, I'm a smart guy, right? I'm using a thin-gauge needle. I'm sterilizing it. I'm not injecting anything. Some diabetics do this every day of their lives to test blood sugar. They're fine, and I'm fine. It's no different than weighing yourself every morning."

"Robert," said Sandra, "You are stabbing your own arm to entertain yourself. You don't find that concerning?"

"Oh, sweetheart," said Robert. "I'm not mutilating myself. This is not a cry for help. I am not channeling my emotional pain. I wouldn't even know I was pricking my skin if I didn't watch my hand. You wouldn't know I was pricking my arm if you hadn't seen me. It doesn't even look like a rash."

"That's not the point," said Sandra.

"Then what is the point?" said Robert. "I am healthy, and I am collecting useful data. Would you like me to be a victim? I am an empiricist. If you understood that, you would set aside these biases; blood is not witchcraft. I am not preparing an elaborate curse. I am not tattooing myself. Let's look at the facts. I bleed longer than other people. Fact. This has only been tested by looking at chemicals in my blood. Fact. I do not seem to bleed exorbitantly. If I'm right, wouldn't that be interesting? If I bleed more at some times than at other times, wouldn't that be interesting? Never mind that it could help thousands. Let's set that aside. Let's forget that. Let's look at my desire to know myself. I'd like to know what my actual tolerances are, wouldn't you? Wouldn't you like to know how careful I need to be? Doesn't that sound better than calling doctors to ask permission? Don't you think?"

"I understand where you're coming from," said Sandra. She smiled, but it wasn't genuine. "Can you reassure me that this isn't going to escalate? You'll stop if you experience unexpected side effects?"

"Oh, sweetheart," said Robert. "Of course. I am not a crazy person. I'm sorry I had you worried." He held out his arms and she embraced him without hesitation.

"You know what would make you feel better?" he said.

"Butter pecan ice cream," said Sandra.

"Mmm. That too," said Robert. "But no. What I think would make you feel better is if you let me prick your arm, so you could feel that it's really not a big deal."

Nothing in the Basement

"No thank you," Sandra said against his chest. "I don't need to be stuck with any needles. Besides, what if you accidentally acupunctured my heart chakra, and I fell in love with someone else, or my kidneys switched places? No."

"I think it would be good for both of us," said Robert. "It would be a real sign of trust."

"So I should trust you, but you don't have to trust me."

"Don't be reductive," said Robert. "Let me prick your arm, and then let's have ice cream. Five minutes, maximum."

"Robert, no," said Sandra. "It's gross. No."

"The human body is not gross," said Robert.

"Oh my god," said Sandra. "You want me to be your control group. That's it, isn't it? You want my data so you can see how it compares to yours, because there's not a table you can check online, because this is not a standard test. Jesus!"

"It would take five minutes."

"Five minutes how many times?"

"Just once."

"Just once until you start thinking that you could use a broader sample. Until you start obsessing over ways in which I sat wrong, or had the wrong heart rate, or maybe I was ovulating."

"More than one test would be nice, if you're offering."

"No," said Sandra. "I will not get caught up in this. I will not let you peck at me with needles until you get the answer you want! No. Stop asking."

"I am simply collecting physical metrics," said Robert. "If you are too squeamish to participate, I guess I have to take that in stride. But I'm very disappointed. Very."

Nothing in the Basement

For the remainder of the evening, Robert sulked. Sandra took the dogs for a long walk because they couldn't run in the back yard. She said that was why. It seemed passive-aggressive, but Robert allowed that she might be trying to cool down. That she might manage to walk herself into a calmer frame of mind, reconsider his proposition.

He was asking such a minor thing. Hadn't he made a thousand little concessions to her pet peeves and preoccupations? Sandra was only a tireless ally in critical moments. She never failed at the big gestures - staying up all night at a hospital or organizing a massive fortieth birthday party – decorating, catering, making introductions between strangers who became friends. She was a champ. She could do what no one else could.

But at the little things – at the little things, Sandra failed. She couldn't act gracious when he bought the wrong kind of lotion-added facial tissue. She couldn't have the game on the radio when she was driving. She couldn't stop herself from straightening the salt and pepper shakers when Robert was mid-meal.

Robert was beginning to think that the little stuff was really the big stuff.

Sandra might still surprise him. She might come back gung ho. He might have to persuade her to wait until her body had relaxed from the walking. He tried to read a chapter of *The Sun Also Rises*, but he mostly scanned the same page again and again. It aggravated him.

The emptiness beneath the house had no thoughts. The dogs barked at it. But it didn't change. The nothing frightened the dogs because it helped no one and belonged to no one.

Chapter 51

When Sandra woke up, she knew she'd been asleep for a very short time. Her head didn't have the heavy grogginess that usually accompanied an unexpected wakeup; she didn't feel as though she was drifting through clam chowder. She hadn't heard a noise. She was simply, abruptly awake; more alert than she'd been in days. She hadn't yet moved. She knew that when she did, she would move very fast. She wasn't afraid. She was very calm.

A mosquito bit her shoulder. She didn't hear it, but she felt it. Mothers could hear the cries of their babies from very far away. That was the tale, at least. Sandra felt called awake by a baby that neither existed nor wanted to exist. A baby was trying to protect its non-mama.

Robert's breathing sounded wrong. Sandra turned her head – smoothly, quickly – to look at him. Her neck must have twisted like an owl's. His hands were curled under the pillow. His face was serene. He was the picture of peace.

"Robert?" Sandra said. "Are you okay?"

He didn't answer.

"Robert?"

He made a sleepy smacking noise with his lips, and curled his knees toward his chest. It was fake. It wasn't how he slept.

Sandra slid out of bed and walked to the bathroom. She didn't have a hand mirror, but she managed to find an old

Nothing in the Basement

mirrored compact. She perched on the counter and angled the mirror on the medicine cabinet until she could sit in the light and look at her back through one mirror pointed at another mirror. On her shoulder, there was a tiny drop of blood. When she wiped it with a towel, it disappeared. No swelling. No scar. No bite mark. Like it had never been there.

She returned to the bedroom. She put on her robe. She stood at the foot of the bed.

"Robert," she said, "how many times? How many times have you done this?"

He half-snored, and shifted. She shook his foot. He moaned and rolled over, eyes still closed. He settled down, his breathing regular.

His hands stayed safely under the pillow. Sandra walked along her side of the bed, as though she was going back to sleep. She reached out, grabbed the pillow, and pulled.

"Jesus, Sandra!" said Robert. In his hands, he held a needle and a stopwatch. She looked at him.

"It was just this one time," said Robert. "I'm sorry. I don't know what I was thinking. I knew it was a bad idea when I did it, and that's why I tried to pretend it hadn't happened."

"How many times, Robert?" said Sandra.

"This is the only time."

"How many?"

"Once."

"Prove it."

"How can I prove that I didn't do something? It never bothered you before. You never saw blood, you never woke up. It didn't happen."

"I didn't see blood and didn't wake up?"

"Christ, Sandra. What do you want me to say. I'm sorry.

Nothing in the Basement

It was stupid. It won't happen again."

The house made a creaking, shuddering sound. Sandra became aware of a shift in the flooring.

"Did you feel that?" she said.

"How could I not feel that?" said Robert.

"There is definitely a slight incline," said Sandra. "I am feeling an incline." Out on the patio, one of the dogs started howling. Trixie, she thought. Serenely, she walked down the stairs. Robert trailed her.

"Sandra −" said Robert.

"Look at the yard," said Sandra. From the dark of the kitchen, the lawn was clearly visible with an open maw much larger than the hole Sandra had first descended. Sandra knew in her bones. It was bottomless. When she had dropped the shovel, it had never hit bottom − only rang as it glanced off the sides. Sandra knew that her body was gobs of raw meat packed around a skeleton. No more, no less.

The porch tilted away from the house at an angle − at a twenty-degree downward slope. Pilgrim, not Trixie, howled in a corner. Trixie paced, growling low in her chest.

"We'll have to move them to the parlor," said Sandra.

"Okay," said Robert. He tried the patio door. It slid an inch, then jammed. "It's stuck," he said.

Sandra took down her iron skillet. "Stand back," she said. "I don't want you to get hit with flying glass." She stuffed her robe with dish towels. She swung as though she wielded a baseball bat. She followed through. She turned the pan so the edge hit first.

Shards slid across the porch. The dogs cowered behind a wicker loveseat while Sandra smashed the pan around the edges of the hole until the lower edge of the door was smooth − no glass teeth. Nothing to snag the dogs. For good measure, she set a cutting board atop the worst of the broken glass. She knelt.

"Come on, Trixie," she said. "Come on, Pilgrim."

Trixie, the braver but more neurotic of the two, came out of hiding first, but returned several times to the safety of the chair. Pilgrim, slow and steady, led the way through the broken door, Trixie following on his heels.

"Good dogs," said Sandra, wrapping her arms around them. "Good dogs."

Robert appeared in the kitchen doorway. He had been securing the breakable objects in the parlor. He felt proud of himself. He was getting things back on track. The dogs saw him, and lunged. Sandra managed to throw Trixie to the floor and pin her there, but Pilgrim surged across the room. Pilgrim leapt for Robert's face. He flung up an arm, and Pilgrim latched onto it, growling. When Robert tried to shake him off, he sat back on his haunches and started to pull.

Robert screamed with the full volume of his minimal theater training. He leaned toward Pilgrim's ears and screamed again. He shoved his arm as far into Pilgrim's mouth as it would go.

"Choke on it!" he yelled. "Choke on it!"

Pilgrim whined, but did not let go. Robert swept Pilgrim's legs out from under him, and knelt on his throat until he released. Trixie was barking frantically. Sandra dragged her to the bathroom and slammed the door. Robert could hear her gouging the wood. Pilgrim panted. His eyes started to close. Sandra grabbed his collar in her fist.

"Get up!" she shouted. She shouldered Robert aside and half-carried the large dog into the parlor. Pilgrim made a gurgling sound. She put an ear to his chest to make sure he was still breathing. When she returned to the kitchen, Robert was gone. She found him upstairs, wrapping his arm with an ace bandage.

"We have to get you to a hospital," she said.

"It's fine," said Robert. "They're not deep wounds. He mostly got bone."

"Damn it, Robert. This is not about your hemophilia. You always go to the hospital for an animal bite. Always." She started to cry. "You could have rabies."

"I don't have rabies. Pilgrim didn't have rabies. I'm in more trouble going to a hospital, if you think about it – I could get a staph infection or something. I already treated the bite with hydrogen peroxide. If I start running a fever, we'll go. How about that?"

"Okay," sobbed Sandra. "Are you sure?"

"I'm sure," said Robert. He put as much confidence into his voice as he could. "Who's more concerned for my life than me?"

"You should get some rest," said Sandra. "I'm going to check on Pilgrim."

Chapter 52

Sandra slept on the sofa in the parlor. All night, Pilgrim wheezed and Trixie scratched at the bathroom door. Sandra found it reassuring; each time she started to wake up, she heard they were there with her, and she relaxed. When she woke up, truly woke, and rose, and confronted the day (early; the windows in the parlor were un-shaded), Pilgrim's head was on her legs. His eyes were open. He licked her knee.

Before Robert woke up, she walked and fed and sequestered the dogs. She started to go through the house, room by room, evaluating the contents for emotional or financial value.

The yard was in bad shape – not a yard, but a void. Sandra was grateful for the warning. In her research, she'd read about a sewage sinkhole in Guatemala, three hundred thirty feet deep. It had swallowed six houses and several people. That had been the first sign that it existed.

Not much was worth saving. It was all nice to have; it was nice to think of a thing and to find it at your fingertips. It was nice to have extra blanket for each kind of weather; it was nice to have extra rooms for guests even if overnight visits were infrequent. Sandra's life had been comfortable. Most of what she owned, she liked. Of her possessions, maybe two percent were priceless - heirlooms, antiques, souvenirs, artwork by friends. History. Maybe twenty percent was garbage: pantry contents, folding chairs, gift bags bought on sale, bulk orders of spare printer cartridges.

The middle seventy-eight percent was trouble. Given a day to sort – and she felt she had a day – it seemed overly dramatic to take only what could fit in a trunk. Outside observers would think she had panicked. Privately, she would know she'd been too lazy to reorganize. That broad middle would have to be sorted and ranked. She would have to settle her estate. She tried to remember how she'd executed her grandmother's. She thought it had involved colored stickers.

When Robert woke up, they both looked at his arm, and Sandra allowed that it seemed to be in reasonably good condition. No puffiness. No angry red streaks. The skin was cool to the touch.

They spent most of the day in different rooms, interacting only to ask about the occasional book, or photo, or piece of marginalia. Robert pulled all the suitcases from the attic. They filled them with small and delicate pieces. Anything larger than a shoe was dragged to a pile in the middle of each room. Upstairs, the floor was treacherously strewn with magazines and craft supplies; Robert had upended any boxes with non-critical material. The cardboard was suddenly more valuable than the contents.

They could have worked side by side. Should have, Sandra thought. As it was, each risked missing things the other one needed. Or loved. She barely remembered to rescue her great grandfather's diary; it had been in a drawer in the office, and Robert was doing the office. Neither had the energy to discuss the events of the night before, or to pretend indifference. Sandra didn't know where to start. Once begun, the fight would unravel into days and weeks.

Nothing in the Basement

Better not to enter into a campaign until you know what you want.

Her phone rang all day, but she didn't answer. She switched the ringer off. When she picked it up to call her mother, she saw many missed calls from work. She lost the motivation to call. She'd show up at her mother's unannounced, or she'd call on the way. Or she'd get a motel. It didn't matter.

At six o'clock, she kissed Robert on the cheek and left to rent a U-Haul. They were out of trucks, so she fitted her car with a none-too-secure trailer hitch and towed a loud aluminum room back to her house. The process took about an hour – fitting the hitch, driving no faster than fifty miles per hour, changing lanes like a grandma with cataracts.

"Let's go," she said to Robert. He was not in the front room. She carried out a chair, and then a suitcase, making as much noise as she could.

"Let's go," she said again.

She found Robert in the basement, unpacking. He didn't acknowledge her. At first, she thought he must have decided not to keep some of the items, and that he was carefully returning them to their places out of habit, the illogical pattern-completion that took over when he was exhausted. Maybe he harbored a hope that they would return to the house, and he wanted to know it would be orderly. Sandra thought he might be making room in the suitcase. But he didn't put in anything new.

"Hey," Sandra said. "We've got to get going. I could use some help getting the heavy things down the stairs."

"I think we're being too hasty," said Robert. "I've thought about this a lot, and, well, I think we're being too hasty. We don't need to leave."

"Of course we do," said Sandra. "The house is going to fall into the ground. That's why we've been packing all day."

"Yeah," said Robert. "But is it? Really? What evidence do we have of that, really?"

"The giant hole in the backyard."

"That's just it," said Robert. "It's in the back yard. It's next to, not under, the house. The patio was in danger, certainly. But the patio was an extension. It wasn't over the foundation. Maybe if there was torrential rain, I'd be worried, but it's not like engineers haven't been out to look at this. Don't you think the soil commission, or whoever they were, would be moving a little faster if there was really cause for concern? Don't you think they'd have told us to move? I think you've been overreacting. Okay, I've been overreacting too. I'm embarrassed, actually."

"Robert," said Sandra, "the house shook last night. The floor tilted. It's falling."

"I think that was just the porch detaching," said Robert. "We'll get someone out to look at it. I won't say it's not expensive, but it's a lot cheaper than giving up on a whole house, don't you think?"

He laughed.

"Okay," said Sandra, careful to maintain an even, friendly tone. "Why don't we forget about packing this stuff. Let's not move anything. I'll go get the big dog carrier out of the garage, and I'll pack Pilgrim and Trixie into the car, and you can work on what you're doing until I come back. If I do that, do you think maybe you'd come to a motel with me, just for a few days, until the surveyors come? Just to be safe. Just because I'm scared, and it would make me feel better? Even if it's silly?"

Nothing in the Basement

"I don't know," said Robert. "We've really made a big mess today, and I'd like to get it straightened out."

"We did," said Sandra. "We made a big mess. Too big to tackle. I'm already pretty tired, aren't you? We can go to a motel, and we can rent a room with a Jacuzzi. We can relax for a while and laugh at ourselves."

"I'm worried about the dogs," said Robert. "What if they bite someone? What if they bite you? I don't honestly know which would be worse."

"They'll be in the cage," said Sandra. "They'll just stay in the cage. I can bring some sedatives – I think I have some left over from Trixie's last surgery."

"I just don't know, Sandra," said Robert. "I'll think about it. How about that?"

"Okay," said Sandra. "I'll just let you think about it for a few minutes." She resolved to go to the garage, get the cage, get the dogs in the cage in the car, and then come back. A strategic retreat. With Robert this wary, persuasion wouldn't stick long anyway.

The house lurched. One wall of the basement snapped into a cobweb of lines. Puffs of concrete powder floated in the air.

"We have to go," said Robert.

"Yes," said Sandra. They walked up the stairs, holding hands. The slant wasn't enough to make them slip, but they could feel it. In the kitchen, Sandra put extra pressure on her left foot, trying to level a balance board. Reflex.

The door from the hallway to the garage wouldn't open. Neither would the back door. Neither would the front door. Sandra and Robert took turns tugging. The house's change in orientation had sent all the door frames out of plumb. The change had wedged their sturdy, weatherproof, energy-efficient doors. They would not budge.

"Okay," said Sandra. "Okay. I'll break a window." But she didn't have to – one window in the kitchen opened out instead of up. It popped loose with a sound that meant it was not going to close again. Sandra used a Chinese cleaver to pry the screen. She had to stand in the sink. Outside the window was an intruder-repelling holly bush. Sandra braced herself and jumped.

"You okay?" said Robert.

"Yeah," said Sandra. "I'm going to try to open this door from out here. You pull, and I'll push."

Sandra ran at the back door several times, but all she managed was to bruise her shoulder. "I'm going to try the garage," said Sandra. "Maybe I can get in and grab an axe."

"I can just climb through the window," said Robert.

"What about the dogs?" said Sandra.

"They can climb through the window," said Robert.

"They're stuck in the guest room," said Sandra.

"Well, that's an inside door," said Robert. "We haven't tried it yet. It's a different situation. I'll check."

"Don't!" said Sandra. The dogs would attack Robert the second they got the chance. She said: "I mean, they're going to be scared, and riled up, and I don't want to chase them through the house. I'd rather get the cage first."

"We don't need the cage," said Robert. "They've ridden in the car without it."

"They need the cage," said Sandra. "I'll be right back. I promise."

The garage door did not want to open. Fortunately, it was made of aluminum, and possessed a flexibility of spirit. On the first remote control push, the door rose a few inches and then jammed. Sandra fetched the jack from her car and expanded the gap. This was enough to clear whatever had caused the first jam. It crumpled part of the door. Upon a second button push, it rose again, briefly, before it froze, shivering, three feet off the ground.

"Good enough for government work," said Sandra. She used her shirt to mop the sweat off her face, not caring if she flashed the neighbors. The street seemed oddly empty. It was twilight, dim enough for street lights. None of the houses had a single illuminated window.

The garage interior looked nothing like itself. To be fair, Sandra's last visit had been a disorderly one – she had overturned several tool benches, as she recalled. This was a testament, she noted, to the fact that there had been tool benches. Now, the straightened benches resembled altars, or islands. They were scrupulously clean, gleaming with a sheen of wet oil. Robert's tools were arranged on the floor in a decorative spiral. The tools were also covered in oil. It was kind of beautiful.

The dogs' car cage squatted between the tool benches, open and inhabited by a yard statue draped with bike chains. Mercifully, it was oil-free. Sandra picked her way through gaps in the oily tool mosaic. Once she had the cage, she used it to plow a clear trail. She had no choice; the cage was too large to loft alone. Once she had it outside, she dragged it back and forth on the grass to get the gunk off the bottom. She fitted the cage into the back of the car, returned to the garage for an axe, decided the axe was too greasy, and settled for a ladder.

Robert was waiting at the kitchen window. Sandra couldn't see him very well – the holly bush outside and the raised floor made for a limited viewing angle. Robert stood several feet back. Sandra could see his eyes and the top of his head. She was grateful that he was tall.

"I didn't hear you close the garage," he said.

"I can't," said Sandra. "It's stuck."

"Well, could you close it?" said Robert.

"No," said Sandra. "It's stuck like that."

"Well, we can't just leave with the garage open," said Robert. "Or the window. God. We might as well put a sign in our yard, saying, 'we're not home, and don't want our stuff. Please rob us.'"

"The house is going to fall into the ground!"

"I don't like the idea of someone walking through my house when I'm not here. You of all people should understand. You wouldn't hire a maid unless you could find one who would let you supervise. Threatened or not, this is our house. It should be decent. Maybe I'm fine with throwing stuff in the ground, but that's not the same as letting vandals in. I'm not talking about recycling. I'm not talking about giving to the poor. I'm talking about teenagers pissing on the walls."

"If this is about your art installation in the garage, I already fucked it up," said Sandra. "It's gone. I dragged the doggie cage through it."

"I don't know what you're talking about," said Robert, which Sandra interpreted to mean that he did – otherwise, he'd say, "what are you talking about?" She put her hands on her hips, then let them hang by her sides.

"The little chapel you built for your motorcycle," she said, "or the garden gnome, or to protect the motorcycle from the garden gnome. It's gone. Please come out and get in the car."

She scrubbed her eyes with the back of her wrist.

Nothing in the Basement

"Not until I can walk out the front door and lock it behind me," said Robert. "Not when people have already broken in and – done what? Meddled with my tools?"

"I never said anything about tools," said Sandra. "Goodbye, Robert." She walked to the car. She waited for him to follow. He didn't.

"If you go," he yelled, "you're going to regret it for the rest of your life."

"The ladder's still there if you need it," said Sandra.

She backed out very slowly, on account of the mostly-empty trailer attached to her car. She expected that at any second, Robert would come out, but he never did.

Chapter 53

Sandra pulled in at the same diner where she and Robert had waited for the plumber the night the sewage line broke. She was already thinking of it in capital letters: The Night the Sewage Line Broke. Like an episode of a black-and-white suspense show. She parked next to a semi truck to make her own trailer look smaller – even dainty. She got hash browns and toast and a milkshake, and then hot apple pie with ice cream. The waitress brought her a cup of coffee on the house.

"You all right, hon?" she said. "You got a place to stay tonight?"

"Yeah. I've got a place to stay," said Sandra. "Thank you."

"Well, you just stay here as long as you want," said the waitress. "I'll get you more napkins." Sandra had gone through most of the contents of the table's dispenser, and her nose felt raw. She thought it probably matched her swollen eyes. She was too chicken to check her reflection in the window. She knew that once she saw the puffiness, she'd have to start the process of tamping it down. She wasn't ready for that. Mercifully, the waitress had brutally shooed any man who tried to tell Sandra to smile, or that nothing in a pretty girl's life could be so bad. The waitress, it seemed, had been there before, or was working on a psych degree in her off hours.

Nothing in the Basement

What am I doing, thought Sandra. She had just left a man to die. That was the straight truth. Maybe he would change his mind and leave – maybe he already had. She had tried to call, but no one had answered. That wasn't like Robert – not even when he was mad. Maybe he'd forgotten to turn on the ringer, or had run out of charge, or had left the house and left the phone in the house. There was no reason to think that the house would go from fine to deep in a hole with no intervening step. Another lurch could startle Robert into sanity, like it had before. That lurch could also dislodge the ladder, or knock furniture onto him. Just as there was not enough reason to assume he would die, there was no reason to assume he would be fine. In her absence, his probability of survival had sharply decreased.

She had left him to die.

He was very ill. No one in his right mind would choose to stay in that house. Sandra had to face that. When she was with him, her judgment was compromised. She was so used to seeing him as the rational one that when he acted strange, she got angry instead of worried. She waited for him to snap out of it. Now, away from him, she could see a pattern. She wondered whether his family had a history of mental illness. He'd never mentioned it. He might not know. His mother was crazy like you said people were crazy, but not crazy like crazy, Sandra thought.

That didn't matter. Sandra told herself to focus. Robert was clearly disturbed. She didn't need to go looking for warning signs. How were you supposed to talk to a crazy person? Did you talk to them like children or adults? Do you accept their delusions – agree you're an angel, or a secret agent, or whatever they need to hear? Do you contradict irrational claims firmly and immediately?

Nothing in the Basement

You don't abandon them, probably, thought Sandra. Robert is non compos mentis. He can't make an informed decision. It therefore descends to me, the spouse, to make a decision for him.

Or Robert is not crazy. He's a fully rational adult making a reasoned choice. That choice will lead to his death. It is not premeditated suicide; he does not himself acknowledge the result of his actions. It is not a decision to join the army or undergo a risky medical procedure; it is not calculated.

To save Robert's life, she should chloroform and drag him if necessary. No measure was too forceful. Maybe he wouldn't talk to her the next day. She didn't want to talk to him. But she'd have done her duty, even if he never snapped out of it. It was the duty of human beings to take care of weaker human beings.

But I'm the weaker human being, Sandra thought. I'm half a foot shorter than he is. What about my duty to protect myself? It was an unworthy thought, and she fought to push it away. Fear was stupid. What had Robert ever done to hurt her? Prick her with a pin? He wasn't violent. If she jumped to the conclusion that he was, then she was the one acting crazy.

Sandra tipped the waitress all the money in her wallet.

Chapter 54

The house was still there when Sandra got back. A part of her had hoped it wouldn't be. The rest of her was relieved, because her body was geared for a fight. As she climbed the ladder, her hands shook.

Robert was sitting at the kitchen table, in the dark. Sandra flipped the light on. He was crying hard. He didn't make a sound. His mouth was open. His breath was shallow. His shoulders jutted forward.

"It's okay, Robert," said Sandra. "I'm back. Shhhh. It's okay."

It took him several seconds to respond. His eyes rolled, unfocused. He straightened, shook his head, huffed twice.

"I killed the dogs," he said. "I don't know. I think it was me. I don't remember it."

"What?" said Sandra.

"I killed them," said Robert. "With knives, I think. There's blood. I'm not bitten. I think I remember something with a knife and fur. I might want to remember so bad that I'm making up memories. Why would I kill the dogs, Sandra? Why would I do that?"

Sandra slammed a part of her mind down. Before she could imagine what had happened. Keep focused, she told herself. What had her great grandfather's war diary said? Confirm that the dead are dead, and work with the survivors?

Nothing in the Basement

"Are you sure the dogs are dead?" said Sandra.

"I killed them," said Robert.

Sandra walked to the guest bedroom and flashed the door open and closed – just enough time to take in the scene. Trixie lay on her side like a damp bundle of furry rags. Pilgrim's head was detached. Sandra didn't see his body. She passed out. When she opened her eyes, she was on her side on the hallway floor. Her head hurt. She'd wrenched her shoulder. When she returned to the kitchen, Robert hadn't moved.

"They're dead," said Sandra.

"God," said Robert. Sandra wrapped her arms around him, ignoring the twinge in her shoulder. It was the hardest thing she'd ever done.

"Let's go," she said softly.

"I can't go out there," said Robert. "I'm some kind of monster. I killed the dogs and I don't even remember."

"I know," said Sandra. "We'll find someone who can help."

"The way Wolf Man could get help? Or Dr. Jekyll and Mr. Hyde? No. There's something very wrong, and it's not the kind of problem the world can handle. Whatever happened started in this house. We have to end it here. We have to ... exorcize me."

"There's nothing to take out of you, baby," soothed Sandra. "There's nothing. All empty. We love science, remember? When we can't explain something, we find somebody smarter who knows more. All those people are out there. We just have to go to them."

"No," said Robert. "They don't know. They weren't here. They didn't believe about the sewage. They didn't believe about the hemophilia. They didn't believe anything."

Nothing in the Basement

"Think about how medicine works," Sandra continued. She found it odd, arguing from Robert's usual position. "When there's an infection, you try to get rid of as much as possible. The body can fight off the rest. That's all we're doing. We're taking you out of this house. We'll leave, and we'll leave this bad stuff behind. We can walk if you want to. We don't have to take the car. We can be naked."

Privately, Sandra was not so sure that leaving the house would solve Robert's problems. The idea of a house infecting a man struck her as far fetched. But well-decorated restaurants were more soothing than prisons. Once she convinced Robert to leave, she intended to get him into the car. With clothes. She didn't know yet where to take him.

"Leave everything behind?" said Robert.

"Yes," said Sandra.

"We'd have to burn it to keep everyone safe," said Robert.

"Then we will," said Sandra. "We'll get some gasoline, and we'll burn the house down." Robert nodded, and she led him to the window. He dropped her hand.

"No – it's no good," he said. He rested his head on the lip of the sink. "I'm infected, Sandra. If I carry it outside, there will be an epidemic."

"No, Robert," said Sandra. "Illness was a bad metaphor." She stroked his back, but he didn't budge. "You're not going to infect anyone," she said. "That's silly. That's like standing too close to a loud speaker, going deaf, and passing on hearing loss. You just need to get out of the house."

"No," said Robert. "Not until I'm fixed."

The house shook again. Sandra's heart leapt. The lurch took forever; they were sliding into the hole for sure. Then it stopped. Sandra felt as though she was pissing out of the pores in her legs. She had to lean against the counter. The house was now off-kilter enough to show the slope. Pictures hung loose from the wall. The pot rack pendulumed until it settled several degrees off perpendicular. The ridge in the kitchen floor was the edge of the hole. *It really is under us,* she thought. If they were lucky, the whole house would shift, and the furniture would coast to the back wall, and plummet to the bottom of a dark hot hole.

"Robert," said Sandra, and her voice was pitched like a hurricane siren, "I can't argue with you. I am going to climb out this window, and you are going to follow me, and if after that you decide to go back in the house, I won't stop you, but I want to finish this conversation on the lawn." She was almost singing on a single note.

"Don't leave me," said Robert.

"I'm not going to leave you. We're going to leave together."

He wrapped his arms around her. She hugged him back. He made choked noises in this throat. He rocked her in his arms.

Only, he wasn't rocking her. He was edging her slowly backward, away from the window. She tried to push off his chest, but he held her tightly. She couldn't get her arms between their bodies.

"Robert," she said. "Robert, let go."

"Don't leave me," he said. "I can't stand it. I'll die without you."

"Let go!" said Sandra. Her feet slid along the linoleum. She swung her arms to batter Robert's back and head, but she could feel what little force she was using. Pinioned as she was, she might as plausibly try to fly by flapping her hands. She tried to grab onto the doorframe as they passed into the living room. Robert didn't even pry her fingers. He just pulled, and she couldn't hold on.

"You're hurting me," she said. He still hadn't tried to harm her – only move her. If he knew he was hurting her, he might let go.

"I love you," he said. "I love you so much."

Sandra's brain sent up fireworks. "He killed the dogs," her brain said. "It's not safe. He killed the dogs; he'll kill you! He killed the dogs. Get out!" Sandra squirmed like an eel. She flung her body in any direction she could, just to build up momentum.

"Remember that time we went swing dancing?" said Robert. "That was fun. I don't know why that went out of style. You had fun, didn't you? In your saddle shoes?"

Sandra was screaming a continuous babble of help-me-get-off-let-go until she couldn't hear the words. The lights were off. Everything in the room looked very bright. They couldn't have fought all night. It couldn't be daytime.

As Robert rounded the bottom of the stairwell, Sandra wriggled her torso free. She stretched out her arm and she grabbed the heavy brass statuette she kept on the table by the front door – an unobtrusive weapon. She grabbed the brass statuette and smashed it into Robert's head.

He went down with a sound like a cow. He landed on top of her. Her spine hit the edge of a stair step. For a paranoid minute, she thought she'd been paralyzed. But no – she was just winded. She flopped under Robert's limp body, trying to wriggle out or push him off. Through the window, she could see it was dark out. It looked so bright – so very bright.

Robert grabbed her throat and held her down. He only needed one hand. He crawled up her body. He held his face over hers. The whites of his eyes had turned red.

"No," he said. "You stay with me."

He lifted her as though she was a bag of grass cuttings. He carried her up the stairs and arranged them in bed, her back to his front. His arms were around her, and one of his legs. He rested a chin on her shoulder. She had forgotten how big he was. He'd been tall, but never sprawling. In all the time they were married, he'd taken up so little space.

"Remember when we tried to go camping together?" he said. His voice was friendly. "It rained all weekend and even though we kept the firewood in the car, it still got too wet to start a fire. Somehow, even in all the rain, a mosquito managed to find you and bite your cheek. Do you remember that, baby? When the mosquito bit your face? It must have had some kind of special aquasuit. You were so mad about it, and I loved you so much. I thought the mosquito made a pretty good choice. I would have flown through the rain if I was that mosquito."

Sandra felt wetness on her ear and along her neck. "Are you crying?" she said. Her throat sounded like it was made of discarded can lids.

"No, baby," said Robert. "I'm bleeding."

"We should get you to a doctor," said Sandra.

"Oh, Sandra," said Robert. "You're not going to trick me with that." He gave her a squeeze. Her whole body was numb.

The emptiness beneath the house had no thoughts. The dogs were dead. It helped no one and belonged to no one.

The dogs barked silently.

Chapter 55

"I hate camping," Sandra finally said.

"Let's not talk about it, then," said Robert. "Remember when I took you to that arty circus for your birthday? And afterward we went out to dinner. Where did we get dinner?"

"Tosca."

"That's right. And you ordered clams and we drank two bottles of wine and you dropped a clamshell in your lap. You just laughed even though there was garlic butter all over your favorite dress. What color was that dress, again?"

"Blue."

"Turquoise, I thought," said Robert. He sighed. "We used to have some good times, don't you think?" Sandra didn't answer. In the silence, she heard a car drive past. Surely, the hole had to be visible by now. The house's predicament had to be obvious. Then she remembered that it was still dark. The driver was either drunk or tired.

"That's all right," said Robert. "I know we had good times. You know, too. You're just being surly, and that's fair. It's been a hard day. It'll get better. Don't you worry. Or worry all you want. I'm not going to tell you what to do. I'm just going to love you, like I promised. That's all." He pressed closer. Sandra hadn't thought it was possible. Underneath it all, she still found it relaxing to be held. She still loved the smell of Robert, and the perfect softness of the bed.

Nothing in the Basement

"It's not a bad place to die," she told herself. "It's what most people want, isn't it? To die comfortable, in my bed, in my house, with my husband telling me he loves me?"

She didn't have another option. She lay quietly as Robert talked. She let her mind drift to whatever subjects caught her fancy. There was no pattern; she'd spend five minutes wondering how a lace maker tatted a particular kind of doily, and then remember an old California Raisins commercial. She worried about whether the passwords to her internet accounts were in a place that someone could find. Would that someone would be a stranger or her mother?

"I should have had a system," she thought. "I always meant to." The sex toy sweep, the magazines called it. It seemed like the kind of responsibility you gave your kids' godparent. That was one thing Sandra regretted – not being able to tell someone she trusted them with her child. There wasn't an equivalent gesture.

Her back was very warm. Maybe Robert had a fever. Then again, it was summer. She was sweating. The blanket underneath her felt wet. She wished she could change her shirt.

"... so funny sometimes," Robert said. He had started to slur his words. "I can't even explain what makes you so funny. It's just you. It's who you are. I can't understand why people don't laugh at you all the time. I mean in a nice way. The way you sneeze or take a drink of water. Do you remember that party where that guy was hitting on you and you started saying ridiculous things about basketball just to see how far he'd go with it? When he wasn't watching, you shot me this look. Like we were the only ones in on the joke. I think of that sometimes, just out of the blue. I just start laughing. People must think I'm crazy. Nobody else..."

Nothing in the Basement

Sandra drifted in and out of dreams about the Sunday school where she'd gone with her grandmother during a brief stormy period. Her grandmother had tried to "save" her and her brother in a war against her father. The memories all tangled up with puberty. So were the dreams – repetitive awkward dances in the sanctuary; she neither touched nor looked at her partner. Once she was deep enough in the dream, she would shift her real-world body. Robert would hold her still, and she would jerk awake.

"Don't fall asleep," she told herself. "You have to outlast him." Then her eyes would ease shut and she'd think: "What's the use? You might as well die asleep and not notice." Both the dream and waking from the dream were tedious.

Sandra didn't know how much time she passed that way. She'd always banned light-up clocks from the bedroom; she couldn't stand seeing the glow through her eyelids. After an uncountable interval, she found she could move just a little. She didn't try to move. She didn't push to see how far she could get. She wasn't sure how she knew she could move at all. But Robert was relaxing.

"I get scared sometimes," he said. He was hard to understand. It sounded like he wasn't opening his mouth all the way, like he was talking through a mouthful of spit. "I get so scared. Scared like nothing is right. And I wish you would comfort me. I wish you would be nicer to me. I don't understand. It seems like it wouldn't be hard. And you don't do it and it scares me to think you won't ever."

Sandra waited and listened. She tried to remember nursery rhymes she'd liked as a kid, jump rope hand claps about Miss Suzie. She counted to five hundred and back again, and back through the nursery rhymes. Little Jack

Nothing in the Basement

Horner sat in a corner. The owl and the pussycat went to sea. She waited as long as she could wait. She waited until a voice in her head said she'd be a fool to fall into a hole on account of patience. She had one chance, she thought.

She burst out of bed. Robert's arms slid off her with no fight; it was as challenging as taking off a dress. When he made no move to grab her – no sound of motion – she looked back and saw that the bedclothes were soaked in blood. Parts of Robert's face were white. Others were grayish purple.

"Where are you?" said Robert. "I can't see anymore."

Sandra stripped off her clothes and dropped them on the floor. She pulled on a sundress which could be slipped over the head and loafers that required no socks. She didn't trust herself with fasteners. Robert was calling her name. She looked at him one last time. She wanted to kiss his forehead and tell him she loved him, but she couldn't make herself risk it.

On the climb downstairs, she was careful not to trip on any beads or papers. The ladder was where she left it. She'd been afraid it had gone, down the hole.

The keys to her car were still upstairs. She walked to the garage and rolled out the motorcycle. Its key was hidden in a jar of loose nails. As these things were.

She walked the bike to the end of the driveway. She stood in the road wishing a car would drive by.

"It should be morning now," she thought.

No one drove by.

Sandra pointed the Triumph down the center of the road and depressed the accelerator as far as it would go. The important thing was to depart as quickly as possible. Go until she hit a wall or ran out of gas.

About the Author

Romie Stott (pronounced like Romeo without the ending o) is an editor at the Hugo, Ignyte, and British Fantasy Award-winning magazine *Strange Horizons*. Her short stories, poems, and essays have appeared in *Analog, Arc, The Deadlands, Atlas Obscura, The Toast,* and *On Spec*.

As a narrative filmmaker (working mainly as Romie Faienza), Romie has been a guest artist at the Institute of Contemporary Art (Boston), the Dallas Museum of Art, and the National Gallery (London). She is the writer/director of the feature film *Hayseeds & Scalawags*, and is the book writer of the musicals "First, Contact" and *The Lady Takes the Mic*.

Romie is a Texan who lives in Massachusetts. In her day job, she creates closed captions for live television. In the evenings, she is half of the electronica duo Stopwalk.

www.ingramcontent.com/pod-product-compliance
Lightning Source LLC
Chambersburg PA
CBHW070703280626
47159CB00022B/1838